I0646256

Seeking Sarah

Pamela Lamb

Agneau Press
2010

First published 2002 by Agneau Press,
Email: agneaupress@optusnet.com.au

Reprinted May 2010

Cataloguing in Publication Data
National Library of Ausralia
Lamb, Pamela, 1949-.
Seeking Sarah.

For secondary school age students.
ISBN 0-9580489-0-8.

1. Teenagers - Fiction. 2. Floods - Queensland - Ipswich -
Fiction. 3. Interpersonal relations in adolescence -
Fiction. I. Title.

A823.3

Edited by: Sandi Jones
Cover design by: Chris Platt

In memory of my father
Thomas Edwin Lamb
1914-2001

A life well lived

1

In the hush of a hot afternoon two girls stood in a small bedroom. The sun forced its way through heavy lace curtains to lay long, golden fingers on flower patterned wallpaper and reveal grey dust on the mosquito net looped up over the big wooden bed. From the school across the street came the sound of ball on bat, loud in the still air. An insect chirped in the creeper outside the window.

One girl, the taller of the two, wearing a white muslin dress and a pair of old elastic-sided boots several sizes too big for her, stared down at the small red leather book held in her hand.

"But this is *your* diary, Martha. You've already started writing in it. Why do you want to give it to me?"

Martha flicked a strand of dark hair over her shoulder.

"They always give me diaries and I never keep them. Why should I? Nothing exciting ever happens to me."

"*I* happened. Wasn't I exciting?"

"Yes, and I've written about you! But now ..."

"I'm not exciting any more."

"Don't be silly, Sarah. It's just that it's *you* that everything's happening to, not me. I thought you should be the one to write it down." Martha took a step forward. "But first I've got to show you the hiding place. Give me the book!"

There was a small fireplace on the wall opposite the door. The grate was empty. Martha crouched down and reached carefully into the chimney.

"There's a shelf, see? Just within reach." She pulled her arm out and stood up. "Now see if you can find it."

Sarah glanced down at her white dress. "Won't I get dirty?"

"Not if you're careful. The shelf's on the left hand side. No, a bit higher. There, that's right. Can you feel it?"

Sarah's hand touched the soft leather cover of the diary. "But why do I have to hide it?"

"Because otherwise Bertie'll read it. Beastly little toad! Just be glad you don't have a little brother, Sarah!"

Sarah stared down at her sooty fingers. "I can't imagine writing anything that has to be kept a secret."

"What about who you are? Where you come from? You don't want everyone knowing about *that,* do you?"

"Oh, yes. I'd forgotten."

"Honestly, Sarah, how can you have forgotten? You've only been here a week. Now let's go and wash our hands. Papa'll be home soon and he'll want his tea."

"Come on, Kirsty, hop up out of the way."

My mother advanced towards my bed, her arms full of old sheets. Behind her I could see David, her architect boy-friend, armed with chisels and hammers, and I knew there would be no more peace.

"What is it this time? In *my* room?" I stuck a mark in my book and swung my legs over the side of the bed.

"We're going to uncover the fireplace. Won't that be nice? Your own fireplace!"

"In Queensland? You've got to be kidding!"

My mother shoved her way past me and began covering the bed with the sheets.

"Come on, Kirsty, for heaven's sake. You spend far too much time up here as it is."

"It's what I'm supposed to do. What you told me to do. I've been sick, remember?"

But it made no difference.

"Go downstairs and get yourself a can of soft drink, Kirsty. It's cooler down there, anyway."

On my way downstairs I stood on the half-landing, listening to the sound of banging and thumping coming from my bedroom. The light was silver-cool coming through the small round window set in the wall. In the afternoon, when the sun came around the side of the house, it was full of coloured light. Coloured light from a plain glass window. I hadn't worked out why, only that it made me feel good to stand there with the warm light all around me.

The kitchen was pure '70s - lime green laminex and pretend pine - but it would be some time before anything could be done about it after the expense of making over the small back bedroom into a bathroom. Of course, claw-foot baths and authentic black and white tiles don't come cheap and, of course, Mum had to have them. Not that I had any objection to the bathroom itself. The alternative was a shower and toilet in the laundry outside the back door, a room which had been doing double-duty as a store for old beer bottles and damp newspapers when we moved in.

We'd been in the house for six months, ever since my mother took the chance of a junior partnership in a local accountancy firm and moved us up from Melbourne. I suppose she was in the mood for change, having split from my dad several months before, and the mood persisted long enough for her to fall in love with this old wreck of a house - a two-storey stone cottage, heritage-listed with the council and ridiculously expensive.

And now here we were in October and the whole year lay in ruins behind me. Not just Mum and Dad, though that was bad enough. But I'm a swimmer, see? With shoulders like mine and boats for feet, there wasn't much else I could be. And I had missed out on a place in the zone squad; missed by a whisker, my coach said, which was supposed to make me feel better about it. I'd have been all right if we'd stayed in Melbourne. But Queensland kids are born swimming and against them I had no chance.

Then I got sick and spent a week in hospital nearly dying from a chest infection that didn't seem to want to respond to the drugs they gave me. At least I found out what I had to do to get my mother to stop working and pay me some attention. Though nearly dying is an extreme form of attention-seeking in anybody's language.

Late in the afternoon Mum and David called me upstairs. There was dust everywhere, shimmering like gold in the sunlight coming through my window. A pile of rubble lay on an old sheet. Roughly exposed in the middle of the long wall opposite the door was a small oval fireplace. It had a pretty carved mantelshelf and what looked like tiles around the outside but everything had been painted thickly with green paint. The fireplace itself was filthy dirty.

David had his arm across Mum's shoulders. "We're hoping that the tiles are original. If so, they'll be patterned but it's going to be tricky getting all that paint off without ruining them. "

Mum ran the heel of one dirty hand through her hair. "We're going to have a shower then we're going out for a meal. Do you want to come?"

I shook my head. "No thanks. I want to have an early night."

A quick glance between the two.

"I suppose we'd better clear up then." David gathered up the sheet of rubble and carried it, Santa-style, down the stairs.

Once they'd gone out I went into the kitchen looking for something to eat. There was some left-over pizza in the fridge so I had that, followed by a bowl of ice-cream. I sprawled in front of the TV until sleep tugged at my eye-lids. Then I went to bed. It must have been about half past ten.

I slept deeply for what felt like hours and woke suddenly to the sound of a car door in the street outside. For a moment I lay stunned, not knowing where I was.

The room swirled and settled. The sound of piano music drifted through the silent house, the melody as familiar as breathing. The echo of girls' laughter.

The moon was full, casting long silver shadows across the floor. I lay still, listening to the old house creaking around me and our resident possum thumping and scratching on the roof above my head. A sound that became more frenzied, as if the creature was trying to gain a foothold, followed suddenly by a soft whoosh! A black cloud issued from the fireplace and spread across the room, blotting out the moonlight.

I reached out and turned on my light. A pile of soot lay on the floor in front of the old grate. Soot hung suspended in the air, landing like delicate rain on floor and furniture. Spiders webs like black filigree decorated the corners of the room

4

"Are you all right?" Mum stood in the doorway with David behind her. He had his tie off and his hair standing on end. Mum started to laugh. "Oh, no! Look at you! What a *mess*."

I spent the rest of the night in Mum's bed and enjoyed the look of disappointment on David's face who obviously had similar plans.

In the morning, while Mum slept, I returned to my room to survey the damage. The pile of soot had settled during the night, spreading itself out across the wooden floor. There seemed to be something else there, something solid. I reached finger and thumb to lift it out.

A book. Or what was left of one. A cracked leather cover coming unstitched from a clump of pages, stuck together with dust and damp. I carried it downstairs into the kitchen and dusted it carefully. The pages at the front and back were ruined but the ones in the middle were not too bad and I found that I could get them apart by sliding a knife carefully between them, one by one.

It seemed to be some sort of diary. Pages and pages of hurried, cramped writing. The first date that I could make out was some time in October. October 1892. I glanced up at the calendar. Same month but more than a hundred years ago. I bent my head and began to read.

"16th October, 1892.

Today Martha's mama took me to visit her sister in Wharf Street to see if she had any cast-off clothes. It was the first time I'd been in town since I got here. I met Martha's cousins, Lizzie and Daisy! I've often thought I'd like to have a sister but now I'm not so sure - ."

The footpath was busy with women going in and out of the shops or gossiping in shady corners. Young lads in heavy jackets and flat cloth caps dodged in and out of the crowds. The street was full of heavy carts and quick, light carriages, people on horseback and pedestrians dodging from one side of the road to the other. The smell, overpowering under the hot sun, was of horse droppings and wood smoke. There were other smells too - grain and soap and sweat and beer and some heavy musky smell from whatever it was that the men put in their hair.

As they approached Mrs Sangster's house a train passed over the stone bridge which spanned the road, billowing clouds of sooty smoke which caused Mrs. Greenaway to tut-tut and shake out her skirts.

"Now look at us! If it isn't the dust, it's the smoke. Nobody would believe we set out clean."

She marched up the narrow path and knocked sharply at the front door. It was opened by a small dark-haired girl with a white face, streaked with tears, who showed them into the front room and then disappeared up the hall.

The room was small, crowded with furniture and very stuffy. Books and magazines and bits of sewing were strewn about. A small woman, sitting by the fireplace on the far side of the room, stood up as Mrs Greenaway and Sarah came in. She had greying fuzzy hair, twisted untidily at the nape of her neck, and a round face with red lips and bright eyes. She was having trouble keeping a crumpled white blouse fastened across her ample chest. She began flapping around the room tossing things off the chairs so that her visitors would have somewhere to sit.

Mrs. Greenaway, taking no notice of this display, marched across the room and sat down in a straight-backed chair with a threadbare velvet seat.

"I see Doris still has the toothache."

"Oh, yes, yes." Mrs. Sangster came to rest finally in the chair she had started from. "I've got it packed with cloves. And she puts hot cabbage leaves on it at bed-time. But it's not getting any better."

"Have it pulled. The sooner the better. It's not going to get better by itself, is it?"

"But, sister, the expense! It cost me five shillings the last time I had a tooth out."

"Cheaper in the long run than paying her wages to do nothing but cry her eyes out."

Mrs Greenaway crooked her finger to Sarah, still hovering at the doorway. She turned to her sister.

6

"This is Sarah. She's the daughter of an old friend of Mr. Greenaway's. Up from Melbourne."

"How d'you do, my dear?" Mrs Sangster's eyes were alight with curiosity. "Come up for the holidays have you? I'll have to introduce you to my girls. There are always lots of larks at Christmas time."

"It's the girls I've come to see, sister. They might have some things that Sarah can have. She's lost her luggage and she won't fit into any of Martha's clothes."

"That's your Christmas muslin!" Mrs Sangster was staring at Sarah's high-yoked white dress.

"Well, she has to wear something! She came to us with nothing but what she stood up in. And *that* was hardly suitable."

"But six yards of Swiss muslin, my dear! What will happen when you go up to the Downs? What are you going to wear?"

"Last year's muslin, I daresay. I'll put a new collar on it. I got a nice bit of lace from Richey's last week."

"Oh, dear. A new collar won't do much for it." Mrs Sangster clambered to her feet. "I'll get Doris to put the kettle on. The girls'll be in shortly. They've gone into town on a message."

At that moment there was a loud commotion in the hall, doors banged and two girls burst into the small room, flung their hats from their heads and sat down heavily on the sagging sofa.

One of them got up immediately, extracted a bit of knitting from where she had been sitting, and sat down again.

"That's my knitting," said the other girl, snatching it from her. "I wondered where it went!"

Sitting side by side it was obvious that the two girls were sisters, both having the same brown, almond-shaped eyes set in oval faces with broad foreheads and pointed chins.

The older of the two, Lizzie, had smooth black hair parted down the middle and fastened in a long, thick plait down her back. Because she had reached the magical age of sixteen, she was wearing a plain white blouse with a lace collar and a brown gored skirt, both of which garments seemed to be designed to show off a large chest and tiny waist, things which younger girls in their muslin frocks and flannel petticoats were not supposed to have.

Daisy, the other sister, was plump all over like her mother. Her hair was brown, thick and curly and held in place by a velvet ribbon.

The door opened again and the little servant came in with a heavy tray of tea things which she carried carefully across the cluttered room and placed on the small table next to Mrs. Sangster's chair. She was still crying and as pale as death.

"A piece of twine around the doorknob might be worth a try." said Mrs. Greenaway, just as the girl went out of the door, which made her sob all the louder.

After tea, Mrs. Greenaway stood up and brushed down her skirt.

"I have to be off," she said. "I've told Martha to come over here after school so she can fetch Sarah home. But just remind her she's got her piano practice to do. I don't want her dawdling in town."

When she was gone, Lizzie and Daisy dragged Sarah up the stairs to their bedroom and began pulling out clothes and piling them on the bed. They argued about what she was to have. Lizzie was quite happy for her to have anything that *she* didn't want which pleased Daisy not at all, even though she had already said several times that she was not interested in Lizzie's cast-offs and didn't see why she should always have to wear other people's clothes, just because she was the youngest.

The pile of clothes grew and shrank as Lizzie put things onto it and Daisy snatched them off. The end result was a cotton nightdress with pearl buttons, a liberty bodice with broken suspenders, which neither of them wanted, and an old straw hat in need of new ribbons. Lizzie added a bunch of artificial flowers, slightly squashed, which made the hat look half-way decent and almost changed Daisy's mind about letting Sarah have it. Before she could snatch the hat back, Martha came in and sat down heavily on the bed amongst the discarded things.

"Your ma said you were looking out some things for Sarah," she said to Lizzie. "What have you given her?"

A quick glance between the sisters. "We haven't sorted it out yet."

Martha climbed off the bed and began working her way through the piles of clothes. "These are all *old.* You can't expect her to wear these! We're going to *Penzance* in a couple of weeks. Give her that dress with the pale green stripe, Lizzie, you neither of you like it." She pounced. "And this white blouse with the pretty buttons. It was new last year! I know it's got a tear in it but I'll get Meggie to darn it. And what about some drawers? You can spare a pair each, can't you? She's already got a pair of mine!"

Ten minutes later she had assembled a pile of clothes that included several sets of underclothes, a couple of blouses, a navy blue pleated skirt and the pale green dress. She added the disputed straw hat to the top of the pile.

"You'll have to let her have the hat," she said to Daisy, "to cover up her hair until it has time to grow."

"Yes, what happened to your hair?" asked Daisy. "Did you have nits? They must have been very bad to have it all cut off."

Sarah rubbed her hand across her short blond curls but it was Martha who answered.

"Sarah's been sick. *Very* sick. Melbourne's too cold for her. That's why she's come up to us for a while."

"Did you come up on the train?" asked Lizzie. "Is that how you lost your luggage? The railways are always losing people's things."

"I bet you've got some nice things, Sarah!" said Daisy. "Melbourne has much better shops than Ipswich."

"That wouldn't be hard," said Lizzie. "Ipswich hasn't *got* any shops. Not ones you want to go into anyway. Whereabouts in Melbourne are you from, Sarah?"

Again the helpless look between the two girls.

"Oh, leave her alone, you two," said Martha. "Come on, Sarah, let's go home. I've got my piano practice to do. Doris can bring the clothes up to our house tomorrow after she gets her tooth pulled."

They clattered down the stairs and Martha called, "Bye, Aunt Bet!" through the parlour door.

But they were not so easily rid of the other girls. The four girls walked under the railway bridge and set off in the direction of the town centre along a road that followed the river. On one side of the road stood old buildings with empty windows staring at the sky. On the other side the river flowed, sluggish and brown, past sheds and wharves as derelict as the buildings. The timber was grey and dull with age, boards were missing, steps broken. Two bare-foot boys sat on the edge of one of the wharves, a tin bucket between them, fishing in the river. On the far side of the river thick green bush grew to the water's edge, loud with insects.

"What used to be here?" asked Sarah, interrupting a flow of conversation which had been taking place between the two sisters ever since they left the house.

"Wharves," said Lizzie.

"Yes, I can see *that*. But what for? And what happened to them?"

"They were for the steam boats." said Martha. "They used to run between Brisbane and Ipswich. Lizzie's grandfather was the captain of one."

"The *Emu*." said Lizzie. "That's what she was called."

"So what happened?"

"The railway went through. That's what happened. About thirty years ago. Nobody wanted to go by steamer after that."

They turned into the next street, away from the river, and walked along past the shops.

"You'll never guess who we saw today," said Daisy, linking arms with Martha. "Arthur Duncan! Coming out of the bank."

"I saw him first," said Lizzie. "At least, he saw me. It was me he spoke to!"

"I'm not surprised he saw you," said Daisy, grumpily. "With that chest of yours sticking out all over the place."

Martha pulled a face. "Arthur Duncan! I remember him from school."

"Well, he's not in school any more," said Lizzie. "He's got a job in the Building Society with Papa."

"Yes, I've seen him," said Martha. "He's got a faceful of yellow whiskers. Not my idea of a man. *And* he wears cardboard collars."

"Just because you're going up to Toowoomba while we're stuck down here in Ipswich," said Lizzie. "We have to take what we can get."

"Is that where we're going?" Sarah said to Martha. "But what's this *Penzance* place your mother was going on about?"

"It's my grandmother's property. We always go there for Christmas."

"Yes and it's not fair," said Lizzie. "The best social life in the whole colony. Balls and racing and visiting. Squatter's sons! And now Sarah's got my pale green dress. It'll go to *Penzance* and I've got to stay home. It's got mutton sleeves, too!"

"Our Jimmy's told us all about it," said Daisy, who had paused for a moment to look at herself in a shop window and adjust the angle of her hat. "So we know what it's like."

"Oh, yes. Jimmy," said Martha. "I heard he was back. How is he?"

"Papa's got him a job in the police force," said Lizzie, "He's gone to Brisbane to do some training."

"I wonder how long that'll last! Jimmy's their brother," Martha said, turning to Sarah. "He's been up at *Penzance* learning to be a stockman. And what was it before that? 'Prenticed to the woollen mill, wasn't he? That would have been a good job, if he'd stuck it out."

"Yes, but it wasn't his fault he had to leave the mill, Martha! The wool made him sneeze."

"And it wasn't his fault he got sent home from *Penzance* either," said Lizzie. "Everyone always blames our Jimmy! Just because he was learning to handle a whip."

"Yes, but whose nose was it that he nearly took off?" said Daisy, walking backwards along the footpath. "Drew Greenaway! The boss's son. Martha's *sweetheart*!"

"He's my *cousin*." Martha had gone red.

"Maybe he is! But you're still sweet on him. Tell me you're not!"

Martha turned to Sarah. "Wait until you see him! *Anybody* would be sweet on Drew Greenaway!"

Daisy, still walking backwards, bumped into a plump gentleman with a round red face and white mutton-chop whiskers who turned out to be her father on his way home from work. He raised his hat politely and smiled, showing a neat row of pot teeth.

"Well, now, young ladies!"

Martha smiled back, introduced Sarah and made her excuses.

"He's worse than the rest of them put together," she said, taking Sarah's arm and hurrying along the street. "Once he starts talking you can never get away. And I'm starving!"

2

Mum came into the kitchen, eyes bleary, and reached for the kettle. "Didn't you make any tea?" She carried the kettle to the tap. "What's that you've got?"

"It's a book, a diary. It fell down the chimney with the soot."

"A diary? Let's have a look! " She crossed the kitchen and took the book from my outstretched hands. "It looks very old!"

"It is old." I reached across the table. "Look, there's the date. At the top of the page."

" 1892? That wasn't long after the house was built! Eighteen eighty - something, wasn't it? I never can remember!"

"Eighteen eighty *six*, Mum. It's written over the front door!"

Mum stared down at the book in her hands.

"You see what it means though, don't you Kirsty? Whoever wrote that diary would have been one of the first people to live in this house! I can't wait to tell David! Who wrote it? Do you know?"

"Her name's Sarah. But she's not part of the family. She comes from Melbourne."

"So you don't know who the family is?"

"They're called Greenaway. There's a daughter called Martha. And some cousins that live in Wharf Street."

"It's interesting though, isn't it?" Mum dropped the book on the table and turned around to make the tea. "What are you going to do with it now?"

I reached out and took the book back. Held it in my hands. "I thought I'd transcribe it onto the computer. The bits I can read anyway. It'll give me something to do. That's if it's okay for me to use your study."

Mum carried the teapot to the table.

"That's a good idea. You must be feeling better if you want to do something."

"I *am* feeling better. And if I have to stay home from school ..."

" ... which you do. You heard what the doctor said. For another couple of weeks at least."

"... which I do. Okay, Mum, I'm not arguing. But I have to have *something* to do. It's driving me crazy being home all day by myself. And I've watched enough TV to last a lifetime!"

Mum laughed. "Well, that's an achievement in itself. Just take it easy, that's all. I don't want you getting sick again."

Mum's study was at the front of the house, a cool, sophisticated room with grey vertical blinds, a polished wood floor and the computer workstation tucked in the alcove between the window and the fireplace. Or, at least, where the fireplace would be when Mum and David got around to tearing the wall apart to find it.

It was one of those October days that feel like summer and it was hot by mid-morning. I opened the windows to let in the air, together with the sleepy sound of ball on bat coming from the school across the way. The house was silent, creaking a little in the heat. Starting to read, I soon discovered that Martha's father had been a teacher at the grammar school across the street and had used Mum's room as a study, too. I suppose I had always imagined that it had been a dining room but perhaps the Greenaways didn't have one and ate all their meals at the kitchen table, as Mum and I did. The house must have been crowded at any rate. Apart from Martha, there was a younger boy called Albert - though everyone called him Bertie - and a baby called Ethel. Odd names for kids, I know, but only because they are the sort of names we expect old people to have. But they must have been babies, too, once upon a time.

At six o'clock Mum came home. "I can smell smoke," she said, by way of greeting. "Tobacco smoke," she added.

"Well, it isn't me. *I* don't smoke."

"No, no, not cigarettes. *Pipe* tobacco."

"So what d'you reckon, I've had a man in, or what? I'm not the one with the boyfriend."

14

"No, of course not. Don't be silly, Kirsty. Anyway it's rather nice. It reminds me of my grandfather. He used to smoke a pipe."

"It must have come in from outside. I've had the window open in the study all day."

"Oh, yes, the diary! Did you get much done? What's been happening in the Greenaway house?"

"They've been getting ready to go to *Penzance* for Christmas. I told you, didn't I, they were going?"

"*Penzance*? That's a cattle property, didn't you tell me? On the Darling Downs?"

"Not cattle. Sheep."

Mum rummaged around in the fridge and found a bottle of wine, half empty. She pulled the cork and filled a glass. Sat at the table and kicked off her shoes.

"So tell me! What have they been doing?"

"You've got no idea! Making cakes and puddings. Putting fruit into bottles. They've just finished boiling up a whole pig. And Martha's at the piano practicing the same piece over and over again. It's driving everyone nuts!"

Mum laughed. "Remind me never to complain about Christmas shopping again! But why all the fuss?"

"Mrs Greenaway's father was a riverboat captain. I don't think the Greenaways think she's good enough. She's just trying to prove that she is."

"Poor thing," said Mum, reaching out her hand. "I know how she feels. Your father's family were a bit like that."

"But you and Dad never got married."

"*That* didn't make it any easier. Come on, I want to have a read."

I gave her the papers and she sat at the table sipping her wine and reading the pages one by one. Every now and then she made a comment.

"Who's Meggie? Oh, yes, I remember. The maid. Boiling up a pig's head doesn't sound a whole lot of fun."

And later. "And Walter? We haven't come across him before, have we? It says here Sarah's been wearing his old boots."

I was standing at the bench chopping onions and mushrooms to make a sauce.

"He's Martha's older brother. Studying medicine in Sydney."

"Ah, an older brother, eh?" Mum reached for the bottle and filled her glass. Why's Sarah wearing his boots?"

"Well, you know she hasn't got anything to wear ?"

"Yes, yes, I know that. But why *his* boots? Surely Martha or Mrs Greenaway could lend her a pair?"

"Because Walter's boots are the only ones that fit."

"She must have big feet!"

I turned the heat down under the sauce and sat down opposite Mum. "She's big all over compared with Martha's family. She spends her whole life knocking things over and apologising."

"Well, Victorian houses were very crowded, you know, Kirsty. And not just with people, either. They liked *lots* of furniture in those days. Ask David."

"It's not just that, Mum. She seems so awkward somehow. Out of place. And remember when she and Martha were talking to Lizzie and Daisy? Didn't you get the feeling they were making it up as they went along?" I reached out my hand for Mum's glass and sipped at the cold wine. "And all that stuff about her hair. I didn't get that. What's the connection between short hair and being ill?"

"It's just so they could look after it when they were sick in bed. They used to stay in bed for days - weeks - sometimes. There was no way they could keep waist length hair clean under those circumstances."

"*Weeks* in bed? What was wrong with them?"

"Lots of things. Diphtheria, for one. You had a needle for that when you were a baby. And tuberculosis was a common disease before antibiotics were developed. Scarlet fever was another one. There were plenty of them around." Mum took her glass back. "So maybe Sarah had been sick, just as Martha said. It might account for why she's so vague about things."

"Vague enough not to know which part of Melbourne she lives in?"

"Well, why not? You were pretty out to it yourself for a while when you were ill. I mean, how much do you remember of being in hospital?"

I got up and rummaged in the fridge for salad stuff. "They kept on waking me up and asking my name, I remember *that*. It was very annoying."

"Yes, because knowing *that* and ... and what year it is and things like that is a good sign that you're okay. It's what they do with head injury cases."

"*I* didn't have a head injury."

"You had every indication of one, according to the doctors. Or something very like it. They were talking brain tumours at one stage, you know that. And you had a very high temperature for a while. High temperatures don't do you a lot of good, if they go on for long enough. Which is precisely the point I'm trying to make about Sarah."

"What? That she lost her *memory*? Come on, Mum! That stuff only ever happens in soaps. Not in real life."

"I'm not talking about Sarah losing her memory exactly, Kirsty. I'm just saying it's likely she's been quite ill and now she's in Queensland convalescing. Pretty much what Martha told Lizzie and Daisy, really."

"And, without the front part of the diary, we're never going to find out for sure."

I dumped the bowl of salad on the table and turned to the sink to drain the pasta.

"There is another possibility, you know," said Mum. "It might just be a story."

"A *story*? What do you mean?"

"I mean it's not a diary. Or at least not a diary of real events. Just someone's attempt at fiction."

"But who? Martha?"

"Well, maybe not Martha, either. " Mum took her bowl of pasta. "*She* might be invented, too, don't forget."

"Oh, *Mum*!"

"And maybe not a hundred years ago either, when you come to think about it."

We ate in silence.

Then I said. "You were going to find out who used to live here. When we first moved in. Did you ever do anything about it?"

Mum shook her head. "I didn't know where to begin. But David should know. I'll ask him, if you like."

"Thanks, Mum! At least we'll know if the Greenaways are for real."

"I'll ring him tomorrow."

On Friday evening, Mum came home, trailed by David Whitehead. They came into the kitchen where I was sitting at the table sketching on the back of an old envelope.

"I'm just off for a shower," said Mum. "Help yourself to a drink, David, I won't be long."

David poured himself a slug of whisky from the bottle on top of the fridge, added water from the tap - something which would have made my father shudder - and came over to the table. He peered over my shoulder.

"What's this you're doing?"

"It's a design for that little round window half way up the stairs. I just thought it'd look better in stained glass. That is if it's something we're allowed to do?"

The heritage police, that's what Mum had called David the first time they met. He worked for the council enforcing the legislation which protected the city's old houses from people unfortunate enough to own them and they had sent him along to have a look around our old wreck.

He had advised Mum about the bathroom upstairs and was now heavily involved in knocking holes in perfectly good walls to reveal fireplaces that nobody wanted while he waited for Mum's bank account to recover sufficiently to move on to bigger and better things. Like the lime-green kitchen.

David leaned forward and picked up the envelope. "I don't see why not. It was probably stained glass to begin with. The Victorians were very big on coloured glass." He pulled out a chair and sat down at the other end of the table. "Do you believe in ghosts, Kirsty?"

"*No*! Of course I don't."

David's bland grey eyes stared at me through gold-framed glasses.

18

"So you haven't come across anything ... strange ... since you moved into this house? I'm not talking about ghosts exactly."

"What about tobacco smoke?" Mum came into the kitchen fiddling with an ear-ring. "I didn't know ghost-hunting was part of your job, David!"

David swivelled around in his seat. "It isn't. Not really. What was that you said about tobacco smoke?"

"We smell it in the front room, don't we, Kirsty? At first we thought it was coming in through the window but it's too persistent for that."

"That's exactly the sort of thing I'm talking about! Smells. Or ... or sounds. Although there is a chap - a security guard up at the university. He claims he can see the ghosts themselves. But he's a very unusual young man."

"He's a *nut*!"

"No, no, don't be too hasty, Kirsty. You know what that old place was originally, don't you? A mental hosptal. The Sandy Gallop Insane Asylum, to give it its full title. Built around the same time as this house. There've been too many ghost stories told about that place to explain them all away, however cynical you might be. And quite rightly so, given what went on up there."

"So is there anybody else apart from the security guard who've seen these ghosts?"

"Not the ghosts, no. But sounds. And ... and smells. Most commonly those two things. In one building a door bangs at half past five every evening. My young friend reckons it's the matron doing her rounds. Everyone else just gets freaked out by it. And there's another room in the same building that smells of talcum powder. That room's got photocopy equipment in it now. But it still smells of talc." He placed the envelope on the table, smoothing its edges with a careful finger. "And now we've got the smell of tobacco smoke in this old house. Have you heard, or seen, anything else?"

"Piano music," I said, intrigued despite myself. "The same piece over and over again. And girls laughing. "

Mum's eyes opened wide. "But that comes from next door, surely? Don't, Kirsty! I'll be too scared to sleep."

David laughed. "I don't think there's anything to worry about, Dianne. It's my own feeling that these things are just the remnants of other people's lives. A lot of people have lived in old houses like this one. It'd be strange if they didn't leave *something* behind." He turned to me. "Perhaps one of your Greenaways smoked a pipe."

"The Greenaways!" said Mum. "You've found out about them?"

"No, not yet. That was one of the things I was going to talk to Kirsty about before we got onto ghosts. I'm going to the State Archives tomorrow and I thought I'd look them up then. That's where all the old rates notices are kept, you see, so I can find out who was paying the rates on this place at the time the Greenaways were supposed to be living here. You'll need to tell me the year."

"1892. That's the date in the diary anyway."

"And I need a rates notice with the property description on it."

"There'll be one in the study," said Mum. "I'll grab it for you on the way out. This is very kind of you, David. You'll have to let us know how much we owe you."

"No, no, it doesn't cost anything. And I was going anyway, to do some research for a client. I thought I might take Kirsty along, if she's not doing anything. She might find it quite interesting."

I didn't want to go. Not just because it sounded even more boring than being by myself in the house all day. But he might start up about the ghosts again. I didn't want that. It was bad enough living with them day by day without having to talk about them as well.

"Would you mind very much if I didn't come?"

David looked so disappointed I thought frantically for an excuse. "It's just ... it's just that I want to get on with the diary. It's really interesting at the moment."

"Ah, yes, that's the other thing I wanted to talk to you about! By a strange coincidence I have been asked to inspect a property. An old homestead in Toowoomba. Name of *Penzance*. Ah! I thought that might interest you!"

He turned to Mum. "The new owner's coming up from Sydney with her son this weekend and I'm meeting her on Sunday. Why don't you both come with me? I guarantee it'll be more interesting than a trip to the State Archives."

"Who is she?"

"Her name's Alison Hall. She inherited *Penzance* from some old aunt. I've known about the place for years. So you could say I volunteered my services."

"To do what?"

David grinned. "I want to talk her into restoring the place. It's a wonderful house. You wait until you see it."

"That's where I'm up to in the diary," I said. "The Greenaways' journey to Toowoomba."

"How did they get there?" asked Mum. "It's a long way to go on a horse."

"They didn't go by horse, Mum. They went by rail."

"Quite right," said David, rubbing his hands together. "The railway went to Toowoomba in those days. In fact, the Ipswich-Toowoomba line was one of the first in Queensland!"

"I didn't know you could go to Toowoomba by train," said Mum

"Well, you can't any more. The line terminates at Helidon these days. But it must have been quite a journey!" He turned back to me. "Well, there's no question of me taking you away from your research, Kirsty. Can you print an extra copy for me? I'd love to know what it was like going up the Range in a steam train!"

The following evening David came round for dinner. We had pizza out of the box, sitting in the front room which was marginally cooler than the kitchen. It was one of those ploys that adults sometimes use to manoeuvre kids into a point of view which they might not arrive at naturally.

This one seemed to be all about me seeing Mum's dull boyfriend as an all-right bloke. David played his part well. I doubt if he'd ever eaten pizza before, at least not the take-away variety, but he ate his share and drank several glasses of the red wine Mum provided which was also out of a cardboard box and was definitely not his style.

After we had finished eating, Mum went into the kitchen to make coffee, leaving us to talk. However, it wasn't my game we were playing and I didn't see why I should abide by the rules, especially as David had nothing whatever to say, so I got up and turned on the telly. By the time Mum came back into the room with the coffee things on a tray we were both engrossed in a movie.

At eleven o'clock there was nobody left alive except the rookie cop and the gangster's girlfriend who, predictably enough, fell in love during the last thirty seconds of the movie.

The noise of the credits woke Mum from a doze. "What? What happened? I missed that bit."

"They're all *dead,* Mum," I said, getting up to turn off the TV. "I'm off to bed."

"I'd better be going, too." David got to his feet, yawning hugely. "Thanks for dinner, Dianne. 'Night, Kirsty."

"Hang on a minute, David. Kirsty's got something for you."

I went into the study and came out with a bundle of papers. I held them out to David. "The train journey. Out of Sarah's diary."

David took the papers and flicked through them. "Well, well! An eye-witness account. Not something you find every day. Thank you, Kirsty. I'll look forward to reading it."

Mum and I stood in a huddle on the doorstep, shivering in the midnight air. David walked the few steps down the front path to his car, parked on the kerb. He raised his hand. Then he hurried back to the door. "Forgot to tell you! It's all systems go on the Greenaways." He looked up at the old date carved above the door. "They were paying rates on the place in 1892. A shilling in the pound."

"That's wonderful." Mum glanced in my direction. "Thank you, David."

He grinned. "My pleasure. I'll see you in the morning."

"The Toowoomba train was to leave Ipswich at quarter past ten. At ten o'clock we arrived at the station. Mr and Mrs Greenaway. Me and Martha. Meggie carrying Ethel. Bertie in a new blue knickerbocker suit and a sailor hat, pulling impatiently

at his father's hand. The train was in. A big, black locomotive stood at the end of the platform, steaming gently like some surly monster and behind it half a dozen red-painted wooden carriages with wrought iron platforms at either end. Some people were already aboard, seizing for themselves the coolest seats on the side away from the sun."

Bertie was caught between his desire to get inside the carriage and hang his head out of the window and his need to go up to the front of the train and look at the engine. In the end the engine won and Sarah took him.

They stood and admired the paintwork, the gleaming brass and the glow of the fire when someone in the cabin opened the fire-box door. They looked at the wheels and the pistons and Bertie explained how they worked.

"That's what I'm going to be when I grow up." he said. "My grandfather was a steamboat captain. I'm going to be an engine driver. After all, railways aren't going to go out, like the river trade did." He reached out and put his hand into Sarah's, giving it a tug. "Come on, Sarah. We'd better go."

Sarah looked down at him. A sturdy eight-year-old, untidy as usual and with a runny nose, wiped on the sleeve of his jacket. She didn't know why he'd decided to hold her hand.

She felt an unfamiliar twist of pleasure somewhere in her chest and grinned at him. "Come on, then."

They raced. He won. By the time Sarah reached their carriage, Bertie was hanging out of the window, grinning down at her.

Mr. Greenaway came out onto the little platform at the end of the carriage and they stood side by side for a while, watching the scene. It was a hot day with a warm breeze carrying the scent of the bush to mingle with the normal city smells of dust and horses, and the sharp smell of burning coal from the engine getting up steam at the end of the platform.

"I'm waiting for someone," explained Mr Greenaway. "A lad from school. He'll miss the train if he doesn't hurry up."

Five minutes later, with the engine gasping and sighing and a plume of grey smoke uncurling into the hot air above the station buildings, Mr. Greenaway took his watch out of his waistcoat pocket, opened it one-handed and stared at the face.

"Two minutes," he said, closing up the watch and replacing it in his pocket. "I sent him on an errand. I thought he'd have enough time."

Two minutes later the engine gave a final sigh, steam hissed from the pistons, and the long line of carriages shuddered and creaked and then began to move. Mr. Greenaway leaned over the wrought-iron railing.

"Don't you," he said to Sarah. "You'll get dirty. Not that you won't in any case."

Then a young man appeared, bursting through the crowd of people gathered in the shade of the station building, sprinting up the platform with his hat in his hand, his eyes scanning the carriages for familiar faces.

The train was accelerating and the young man put on a burst of speed, grabbed the hand rail, and swung himself up so that he was standing on the little platform, his face red and streaming with sweat, his collar half undone, and his eyes alight with pleasure.

He grabbed Mr. Greenaway's hand and shook it enthusiastically. "Made it, sir!"

Sarah stared at him. Some school boy! Head and shoulders taller than Mr Greenaway, he had a body like a barn door and a thatch of sandy hair. His too-small school jacket showed bony wrists and large awkward hands. He shoved one hand into his jacket pocket and pulled out a brown paper parcel which he handed to Mr Greenaway. The other hand searched in his trouser pocket and came up with some loose change which he also thrust at his school master.

"Thank you, Angus. This is Sarah." A shy grin in her direction. "Now come on and you can meet the rest of the family."

Angus ducked his head to follow Mr Greenaway and Sarah into the swaying carriage, instantly made it look over-crowded and grinned around with a *let-me-out* look in his eyes. While he crouched on a seat and tried to hide in the collar of his jacket, Mr Greenaway explained.

Angus had left school that day and had planned to return home for Christmas before travelling to Melbourne in the New Year to study law. Angus' home was a vast cattle property in the Gulf country and he had received a telegram from his father's agent in Cairns to say that the trip was impossible because it was raining in the north and the creeks were up...

"... twenty six of them," said Angus gloomily. "Creeks," he added by way of explanation.

"... so Angus is coming to *Penzance* with us," said Mr Greenaway. "Though he may find the Downs a little cramped next to his own place. Oh, yes, and I've got another surprise." He handed the brown paper parcel to Sarah. "These are what Angus nearly missed the train for. So I hope you're pleased with them."

With the eyes of the whole family upon her, Sarah opened the parcel. Inside was a pair of button boots made of soft black leather

Mr Greenaway was looking pleased with himself. "The bootmaker had to make a special last. He's never been asked to make a pair of lady's boots that size before. That's why it's taken so long to get them."

"*Thank* you." Sarah held the boots in her hands.

"Don't thank me, my dear. It was all Mrs Greenaway's doing. There was no way she was going to let you go to *Penzance* wearing that old pair of Walter's."

The train slowed as it began the pull up a long hill which marked the end of the grey bush and the beginning of higher, more open country. Wide fields lay either side of the track. On the horizon lay the flat grey hills of the Divide, hazy in the sunlight. Homesteads and farm properties squatted in black puddles of shade. On one side of the track were fields of sugar cane which was being cut by a gang of big, dark men who straightened up when they heard the train coming and stood waving cheerfully, their smiles white gashes in dirty faces.

"Don't you dare!" said Mrs Greenaway to Martha who only just stopped herself leaning out of the window and waving back.

At lunchtime the train stopped at a place called Bigg's Camp to take on water. Mrs Greenaway handed out corned beef sandwiches and thick slabs of fruit cake.

After they'd finished eating, Bertie and Angus climbed down onto the tracks to watch what was going on at the front of the train. Sarah felt Martha kicking against her ankle.

"So? What do you think?"

"What do I think of what?"

"Of *Angus*, silly."

"He seems nice. And he must be rich." She'd had these conversations with Martha before.

Martha pulled a face. "He's only a school boy, Sarah."

"He's going to be a lawyer."

"When he's a lawyer *and* he's got a coat that fits, maybe I'll take some notice of him."

"What will you do with him then?"

Martha laughed. "*I* don't know. Can you imagine trying to flirt with a great lump like him?"

It was early afternoon when the train reached the high escarpment of the Dividing Range and began to climb. The railway line followed the outline of the hills, occasionally burrowing in tunnels through spurs, or crossing gullies and deep ravines by way of iron bridges. As the train climbed higher Sarah could see beyond the tangled greenery of the hillside to the flat country they had just crossed, misty grey in the heat.

Just when she thought the train could go no further and was about to start going backwards down the hill, it arrived at the summit in a cloud of grey smoke and a great noise of steam. The air was suddenly cooler and rich with the sound of cicadas singing in the trees.

Toowoomba station, a great turreted monstrosity, sat in the middle of a small mean-looking town, made meaner by the enormous width of the streets which seemed to have been designed for a much grander place.

Dust hung over everything, as it did in Ipswich, the big difference being that here the dust was red and had laid a film of colour over everything, from the trees and houses to the horses in the streets which all appeared to be chestnuts.

It suddenly made sense of an argument Sarah had overheard the grown-ups having that morning when Mrs. Greenaway insisted on dressing the girls in white, which was their best, and Mr. Greenaway saying that it was a complete waste of time because who wore white in Toowoomba, or stayed white if they did?

They got down from the train and stood in a huddle on the platform while Mr. Greenaway and Angus went to sort out the luggage. Suddenly there was a loud shout which made everyone turn their heads and there was a young man walking towards them, his hand lifted in a cheerful wave.

Martha gave Sarah a swift dig in the ribs.

"Drew!" she whispered.

Drew Greenaway was about sixteen. He was wearing well-fitting moleskin trousers and a checked shirt with a scarf tucked into the open neck. He was blond, tanned and clean-shaven, the first boy Sarah had met who didn't have a mess of half-grown whiskers on his face. His eyes were very blue

Mrs Greenaway passed the sleeping baby to Meggie, smoothed down her skirts and looked disapproving. But Drew didn't know what disapproval was. He shook Mr Greenaway by the hand, slapped Angus on his back, threw a mock punch in Bertie's direction, kissed Mrs Greenaway on the cheek and grinned at the baby. Then he turned to the girls.

"Cousin Martha! It's good to see you."

Martha pursed her lips together, trying not to look pleased.

"How's your nose? Jimmy said to say he's sorry!"

"It left a little scar. Look!"

Which gave Martha an excuse to stand rather sweetly on tip-toes and examine a small white scar on one side of Drew's nose.

"Come and have a look, Sarah!"

Sarah declined. She could see Drew's scar perfectly well from where she was and didn't need to stand on tip-toe to do so. But that wasn't good enough for Drew. He stepped forward and thrust out his hand.

"You must be Sarah. I've heard so much about you!"

His words were accompanied by a long look from his beautiful blue eyes and a smile obviously intended to melt girls' hearts. He grasped Sarah's hand and held it long enough to make Martha look very cross indeed. "Welcome to *Penzance*," he said.

3

David's information about the Greenaways persuaded me to go on the trip to Toowoomba the following day. If he had told me that Mrs Hall's son was sixteen years old and seriously good-looking I wouldn't have needed any persuasion. But David always did have strange ideas about what were the important things in life.

For some reason I had imagined the new owner of *Penzance* to be elderly and her son middle-aged but I was wrong on both counts. Alison Hall was about my mother's age, a lively red-headed woman with a straw hat on her head, a ring on every finger and a jangling charm bracelet around one wrist. Her son, Greg, was tall and athletic with dark eyes set in a narrow face. His hair was brown and worn quite long.

When we came out of the gloom of the hotel's lounge into the bright sunshine, Mrs Hall was in the middle of some breathless conversation - a one-sided conversation because her son was taking no part in it but was looking around the pretty garden as if seeking an escape route. She stood up abruptly when she saw us, tangling her hat in the large umbrella shading their table, then waved and laughed.

"Call me Allie, *do*! Everybody else does!" she said to me. "And this is my son, Greg. He's been dying to meet you!"

Greg reached up and scooped his hair away from his face. Then he shook my hand and assessed me carefully with his dark brown eyes. He reminded me of Drew Greenaway giving Sarah the once-over on Toowoomba railway station. I wondered suddenly whether Sarah really had disliked him so much. After all, if Drew Greenaway had been anything like as good looking as Greg Hall ... But I had no time for speculation. David was hurrying us all out to his car.

"Have you been out to *Penzance* yet, Mrs. Hall ... er, Allie?" And, when she shook her head, "Ah, well, you've a treat in store. It's a magnificent homestead."

We drove out through the suburbs along wide streets lined with well-grown trees and neat brick houses. Occasionally we caught a glimpse of open country, brown in the early summer heat. The road dipped to a bridge over a gloomy, tree-choked creek and climbed on the other side. At the top of the hill David pulled into the kerb and stopped the car. We all climbed out. There was silence for a long moment

What was left of *Penzance* homestead stood on about an acre of overgrown land surrounded by brick bungalows with neat gardens. It had been handsome once upon a time, a square two-storey house with wide verandahs and a deep roof, sitting to one side of the site, with an unrecognisable ruin next to it, and a huge tree and a large tin shed behind.

There was no need for a key. The door was hanging from its hinges. There must have been a hole in the roof because a shaft of sunshine fell in a bright column down the stairwell, illuminating a large square hall. A carved wooden balustrade went up into the dusty darkness. Doors on both sides led into rooms full of dirt and rubbish. Broken glass was strewn across the floors, together with chunks of crumbling plaster fallen from the ceilings. In one room the french doors were smashed in and there was evidence of a fire in the middle of the floor.

"That's a cedar floor, too," said David in disgust. "Some people!"

We made our way outside. The ruined building between the homestead and the fence was no more than a square pile of rubble. The roof had long since fallen in and dragged most of the walls with it. One wooden doorway was still standing, framing a view of the neat houses on the opposite side of the street.

"I wonder what it was?" said Allie. She was subdued, as well she might be. The place could hardly be what she had expected. Had been led to expect. 'Magnificent homestead' indeed!

The yard behind the house was dominated by an enormous bunya pine. Its roots had humped up under the old paving stones and one of its branches had smashed its way into a window on the upper storey.

The tin shed was full of old boxes and rusty machinery. It smelt strongly of animals - mice or cats, it was hard to tell.

"Or rats," said Greg in my ear, making me jump. "Come on, Kirsty. Let's go back into the house."

At the foot of the stairs I hesitated. "Are you sure it's safe?"

Greg paused. "If we fall, we fall. It'd be better than dying of boredom."

Drifts of leaves, rotten wood where the rain had got in, a scatter of broken glass. In a back bedroom Greg leaned his elbows on the window sill and stared out at the dry paddocks beyond the house.

"What's the idea, Kirsty? Why did your dad get Mum up here to have a look at this place?"

"He's not my dad."

"Step-dad, then."

"He's not even that. He's only my mother's boyfriend."

"Okay, your mother's boyfriend." Greg turned his head. "He told Mum the place was old. He didn't say it was *wrecked*."

"David doesn't see old houses the way we do."

"So what does he see in this place?"

"Its potential, I suppose."

"Its potential? To do what? Fall down in a puff of wind?"

"He thought your mum might like to do it up."

Greg shook his head. "She doesn't have that kind of money. Anyway why would she want to?"

"Well, now you can go back to Sydney and forget about it."

"That's just what I'm gonna do." Greg pushed himself away from the window and turned to face me. Another long appraisal from those deep, dark eyes. "There's only one thing I'd like to move up here for ..."

"I'm going downstairs."

I walked out of the room. He followed. Without another word, we went back to the car and climbed inside.

We had lunch in the dining room at the Hall's hotel. Roast and three veg, and a bottle of wine for the grown-ups.

"Well, what do you think?" said David finally when we had given up on the roast and gone on to apple pie and cream.

Allie laughed. "Admit it, David, it's a wreck! What on earth am I supposed to do with it?" She turned to Mum. "I'm a cook, you see, and I was thinking I might be able to open the place up as a country retreat, you know the sort of thing, and a restaurant. John, my husband, died last year and I've been looking for something to do. We had a restaurant in Sydney, a nice little place, but we had to sell it when John got sick. We'd always run it as a two-man concern, you see, but it was too much work for me alone. That and nurse him. It was cancer, you see, and I nursed him for quite a while."

David leaned forward. "Don't be put off by the look of the place, Allie. It wouldn't take that much work to restore it, really it wouldn't."

"And you're just the man for the job, eh, David? Is that the idea?"

"I won't pretend I've not had my eye on the place for a long time. And, yes, I'd love to get my hands on it. It would be a shame not to at least *try*!"

"Who did the house belong to?" said Mum. "David said an old aunt."

Allie picked up her coffee cup. "It was my husband's grandmother who left it to me. To him, actually, but of course, after he died, it all came to me. And don't ask me anything about her because I don't *know!* I only met her once and that was at our wedding *years* ago. She was really quite elderly - well into her 80s, so I believe. She was in a nursing home when she died, poor old dear, only a couple of months before John. I didn't know anything about *Penzance* until I found a letter from her solicitor in among a whole pile of stuff that had accumulated while John was ill. It seemed like a dream come true ..."

"Yes, but what was her *name?*"

I hadn't realised that I had spoken but there was silence around the table and I found that everyone's eyes were on my face.

"Her name? Lottie Hall. Lottie was short for Charlotte, I expect."

Mum smiled. "What were you expecting? A Greenaway?" She reached out and touched my hand. "A hundred years is a long time, you know, darling. A lot of things can happen." She smiled around the table. "Kirsty found this old diary in the chimney at home. Strangely enough, it seems there may be some connection between our house and *Penzance*. The families who lived in them were related, apparently."

"Really? How *interesting*."

"It's always interesting when you can discover something of the history of these old places," said David. "I'm hoping Kirsty's diary might have some useful information about *Penzance*. That is, if you decide to go ahead with the restoration."

Greg who, having finished his own apple pie, was now eating his mother's, lifted his head.

"What sort of information?"

David considered the question carefully. "That building to one side of the site, for example. It's obviously older than the main homestead. But what was it originally? What was used for? Kirsty's diary might be able to help with questions like that."

Greg turned to me. "I wouldn't mind having a look at this diary of yours, Kirsty." And, in reply to his mother's look of astonishment. "Well, we do own the place, Ma. What's wrong with finding out a bit about it?"

Half way down the Range Mum turned her head to speak to me in the back seat of the car.

"I've got the Hall's address in Sydney, Kirsty, if you want it."

"Why would I want it?"

"To send Greg copies of the diary transcripts. You are going to, aren't you?"

"I suppose."

"He's a good looking boy, don't you think?"

"I didn't think much of him."

"You didn't? Why not?"

"Look, Mum. I just don't like boys who try to sleaze on to every chick they meet. All right? Or do I have to like him because David wants his mother for a client? Is that the idea?"

"Kirsty! I don't know what gets into you sometimes."

"What gets into me is wanting to be left alone to make up my own mind. Is there anything wrong with that?"

I saw David's hand come out and touch Mum on her knee. "Come on, Dianne. Leave it, eh? Let's not spoil a nice day."

On Monday morning I went back to school for the first time since my illness. I didn't touch the diary for almost two weeks until one night when I pushed my homework to one side and took the old book out of the desk drawer. Within the first few minutes I had my answer about the wrecked building at *Penzance* and, by the end of the entry, I had come into contact with Walter Greenaway, the owner of Sarah's old boots, for the first time.

By then it was almost half past ten so I was surprised to hear the telephone ring. I heard the murmur of my mother's voice and then she came hurrying into the study.

"That was David."

"I thought he was in Sydney."

"He was ringing from Sydney, Kirsty. He's just come back from Allie Hall's."

"Mrs Hall's? What was he doing there?"

"Having a meal for a start. You should have heard him raving about it! She's some cook, apparently. But what he really wanted to tell me was that they've signed an agreement."

"An agreement? About *Penzance?*"

Mum nodded. "*He's* going to restore the place to its former glory. Then *she* moves in and starts cooking! They reckon they'll be open for Christmas."

"*Christmas*! But it's nearly the end of October!"

"That's what *I* said!"

"So when are they moving up?"

"Straight away. They should be up here by the end of the month. They've already put their Sydney house on the market. As long as they get a good price for it, they'll have enough money to make a go of *Penzance*." Mum turned to leave the room. "Oh, yes," she said, pausing at the door. "And David says to get your skates on with that diary. He needs your help with the restoration."

"*Me?*"

"Who else? You're the one with the inside information!"

"Well, I've already found out what that ruin was. Does that mean we're in partnership, too? Me and David?"

Mum hesitated. Then she said, "Not just you, Kirsty. Me, too. You see, I've asked him to move in." She took a couple of rapid steps across the room and put her arms around my neck. "You don't mind, do you, Kirsty?"

I shook my head. "David's all right. I like him."

She bent down and nuzzled into my neck. "Oh, it's going to be so good, you'll see. So good!"

I laughed. Wriggled to be free."Get *off!* Leave me *alone!*"

Mum straightened up. Stared down at me. "You're sure you don't mind?"

"No, honest. Why should I?"

"So here we are at Penzance! *Martha and I are in one of the rooms of the original homestead, a four-roomed hut with hessian walls which is where the family first lived when they took up the selection some time in the 1830's.*

Our room is at the front, overlooking the horse paddocks and pastures that slope down to the road. It is a big, square room with a rough wooden floor and whitewashed walls. Martha says it is hot in the mornings because the sun comes right in but it is nicer than the room at the back, where the boys are, which looks straight out on a big bunya pine growing in the kitchen yard."

The big house, built some twenty years ago when Darling Downs society was at its height, had a central front door, a handsome hall, a curving staircase and a number of high-ceilinged rooms all with french windows opening onto wide verandahs. It was a pleasant, elegant house showing the influence of Martha's grandmother who had been a widow for many years and who had run *Penzance* since her husband died, despite the fact that it was her son, Martha's Uncle John, who was nominally in charge.

They had tea on the verandah. The sun had slid down behind the house, casting long shadows across the horse fields. The air was cool, smelling of green water. Swallows dipped and swooped, chasing insects. An old dog sat at the bottom of the steps, scratching and groaning.

After all the greetings and introductions had been done, Grandmamma Greenaway sat down behind a large silver teapot and began pouring tea into delicate china cups which she dispensed to everyone except Bertie and his cousin Jack who were given lemonade and told to run along and sit themselves down on the steps.

Sarah and Martha found a seat on an old cane sofa which smelt of dog but gave them a good view of the various people sitting and standing on the wide verandah. While they took advantage of Mrs Greenaway's distraction to eat a great deal more fruit cake than was good for them, Martha gave Sarah a running commentary on the assembled family.

She pointed out Grandmamma's son, John, who was Mr Greenaway's older brother, sitting at ease in a large canvas chair with his feet propped up on the verandah rail. He was talking to Mr Greenaway, still in his dark school-master's suit and white, high-collared shirt, crouched uncomfortably on a high-backed chair and trying to carry on conversations with his mother and brother simultaneously. John Greenaway was taller and blonder than his brother and had a large bushy moustache through which he sucked several cups of tea one after the other before placing the cup just behind one leg of his chair and pulling out a pipe and a pouch of tobacco.

Drew was leaning against the verandah railing, wet hair slicked back from his face, talking to Angus who was looking relaxed in a checked shirt and a pair of moleskin trousers. Not so bad looking either, Sarah thought, out of that dreadful, ill-fitting school jacket.

The only other person at the table whom Sarah hadn't met was a thin, pale-skinned, serious looking girl who was sitting next to Martha's grandmother. She was the same age as Sarah and Martha but was obviously no friend of Martha's, having greeted her with a rather unfriendly stare from pale blue eyes which had a habit of flicking around from one person to the other.

She was doing it now, flicking from Grandmamma pouring tea and passing cups around, to Mrs. Greenaway sitting at the end of the table with a sleepy Ethel on her knee, to the two little boys wriggling their bottoms on the front steps. And to Sarah. Especially to Sarah.

Well, she was used to being stared at. Her height made sure of that. Sarah stared back and had the satisfaction of seeing the girl's long-fingered, damp-looking hand go up to her neck and finger a large gold cross hanging on a heavy chain.

So this was Martha's cousin, Anne. Sarah had heard her name mentioned many times, usually when Mrs Greenaway was lecturing Martha for being thoughtless and childish. According to Mrs Greenaway, Anne was everything a girl should be, an example of good manners and quiet behaviour which Martha would do well to follow.

Well, she might have wonderful manners, though Sarah, if you didn't count the staring, but she had obviously been behind the door when charm and good-looks were handed out, both of which her brothers seemed to have in abundance. Even little Jack, who was sitting impatiently on the verandah steps with Bertie, waiting for a word from his grandmother that he might leave.

Martha had already told Sarah that her Aunt Alice, John Greenaway's wife, had died when Jack was born and that Jack had a withered arm, the result of it being wrenched almost out of its socket by the midwife in a desperate attempt to deliver him. He didn't look as if he allowed his useless arm to stop him from enjoying life. He was a lively, cheerful looking kid with a solid, country-fed body and a mess of freckles on his face.

"Now don't you boys go too far!" said Grandmamma when the two little boys had wriggled their way to the bottom of the steps to where the old dog stood, tail wagging, hoping for scraps. The boys looked up, their faces two hopeful circles.

"Only as far as the stables." said Grandmamma firmly. "The creek will have to wait until tomorrow. And don't get under everyone's feet!" she called to their disappearing backs.

"There's water in the creek." she said to Mrs. Greenaway. "Jack's been looking forward to a swim."

"But Bertie can't swim," said Mrs. Greenaway anxiously. "I'm not so sure I want him playing at the creek."

"Can't swim?" said Uncle John sitting up suddenly. "What's the matter with the lad?"

"Well, you know as well as I do there's nowhere for him to swim in Ipswich, John," said Mr Greenaway. "There wouldn't be a waterhole within coo-ee after all the dry weather we've been having and you'd hardly expect his mama to let him swim in the river!"

"Then now's the time for him to learn," said Uncle John, rubbing his hands together. "The Condamine's running. I was down there this afternoon. Another good downpour like we had last week and the wash pool will be full."

"What's the wash pool?" Sarah whispered to Martha.

"Uncle John!" Martha raised her voice to be heard. "Sarah wants to know about the wash pool."

"Never heard of a wash pool, eh, girlie?" said Uncle John, pulling his pipe out of his mouth and pressing down the smouldering tobacco with one finger. "Not surprising, being a Melbourne girl. Mind you, there aren't too many of them around nowadays, even in these parts. But I can show you a picture."

He turned to Anne. "Fetch the album, will you, my dear?"

Sitting at the table, they huddled over the big black leather album which was full of photographs held in place by black corners, and dog-eared clippings from newspapers and magazines shoved in untidily. It took Uncle John a while to find the photograph he was looking for, pausing as he went to point out various family members and unfolding some of the clippings to find out why he had kept them.

"Here we are!" he said finally, pointing to a fuzzy picture which showed a mob of sheep being driven into an oblong tank of water set into the ground. There were a great many men standing around. In the background was a large machine which looked like a cross between a tractor and a steam engine. The whole scene was surrounded by thick bush.

"It's a rare bit of history, that photograph." said Uncle John. "Of course, we don't do that sort of thing any more. Haven't for more than twenty years."

"What's going on?" asked Sarah.

"Farmers used to wash the sheep before shearing." Uncle John put his finger onto the photograph. "You can see it here. Through the tank. Into a raining yard. Which is where the engine comes in. Water pumped through pipes. The poor old sheep standing there soaked to the skin. I can remember seeing it when I was a lad."

"Why did they stop doing it?"

"It didn't do the sheep much good, getting them wet like that. They used to lose a few, especially if the weather turned cold. Now we take the fleece off dirty and all the washing and combing happens later at the mill."

"You'll be able to see the wash pool for yourself tomorrow, Sarah." Grandmamma came out onto the verandah carrying a fresh pot of tea. "We're going on a visit to my daughter's house. Martha's Aunty Dot. And the wash pool is on the way."

The next morning, after a large breakfast of lamb chops and fried potatoes, Sarah and Martha got into the back of the carriage waiting at the front door of the homestead. With her black silk bonnet fastened firmly under her chin, Grandmamma climbed onto the box next to Mama.

She picked up the reins then turn around to smile at Sarah. "The wash pool is just at the bottom of the hill," she said, pointing to a line of dusty grey-looking trees.

At the bottom of the slope the track went across a sandy creek bed but, before they got to the crossing, Grandmamma twitched the reins and set the horses going on the rough grass alongside the trees. After a while the carriage stopped, the horses dropped their heads to feed, and everyone got down. They had come far enough to be out of sight of the track and the swell of the hillside behind them hid the homestead from view.

Grandmamma adjusted her bonnet, picked up her skirts and took off into the trees along a path that was almost invisible in the grass. The path led to a wide clearing in which remains of the old yards were visible although overgrown with tall grass and half-grown saplings. The crowding trees kept out the sun, giving the place a gloomy, cathedral-like feeling. In the middle of the clearing, the creek had been widened into a long, narrow pool through which water was trickling quietly. They went through the grass and stood in a row at the edge of the pool, peering down. The pool was half full of black water, smelling richly of decaying vegetation and reflecting faithfully the ring of trees that surrounded it, and the pale oval of Sarah's face.

"Another storm and it'll be deep enough to swim in," said Grandmamma. She smiled at Sarah. "Seen enough? So, we'll be on our way."

They arrived at their destination two steps ahead of a shower which swept unexpectedly from the west just as the carriage arrived at the door of a large house set in pretty gardens. There was a man standing by the open door watching their arrival. He was a squat, strong man with a broad chest and a red face which he mopped with a silk square taken from his jacket pocket. He looked about fifty years old.

He seemed to be highly amused by their wet state and even more amused by their attempts to get down from the carriage and into the house while a pack of dogs, which had come around from the side of the house, tried to jump up and put their muddy paws on their clean dresses.

"Come in, come in!" he said loudly, rubbing his hands together. "Get off, now!" To the dogs, flapping at them with a big, meaty hand.

He put an arm across Mrs Greenaway's shoulders, which she clearly didn't like, and led her across a wide tiled hall into a pretty little room near the back of the house. Sitting in a carved chair by the window, her head bent over a piece of sewing in her lap, was a young woman. She looked up and climbed to her feet. She was heavily pregnant.

So this was Martha's Aunty Dot who was Mr Greenaway's younger sister. She was like enough to the dark side of the family to be almost Martha's twin. And that old red-faced bloke who had let them in was her husband, Eric Potter. He came near enough to patting Mrs Greenaway on the bottom as he propelled her into the room then he pecked his wife on the cheek and went away.

Grandmamma took her daughter firmly by one elbow and sat her down.

"You should be in bed. Now, where's the bell? I'll ring for tea."

After a while, bored with tea-party chat, the two girls made their excuses and went through the open window into the garden. The rain had stopped and the air was fresh although the heat and humidity were lurking not far away. The garden was laid out with gravel walks between beds of flowering shrubs.

The two girls sat down on a wooden bench set somewhat unevenly among the roots of a large poinciana tree in full summer bloom.

"Is that really her husband?" asked Sarah, picking up one of the big red flowers that was lying on the bench.

Martha pulled a face. "Uncle Eric? Isn't he *dreadful*! He'll want to pat me on the bottom, I daresay, before we go home. And you, too, Sarah. I saw his eyes light up when he saw you so don't say I didn't warn you."

"What did she marry him for? I mean, he's pretty old, isn't he? Apart from being revolting"

"What do you think she married him for? Because she didn't want to be an old maid. And he's got plenty of money." Martha bent down and picked up one of the big red flowers littering the ground and tore it to shreds between her fingers. "He took her to Europe for their honeymoon. They were away for almost a year. And you should see her clothes! She's got more pairs of gloves than I've ever had in my life!"

"Yes, but how can she stand it? Being married to someone like him! I mean, does she love him?"

"How should I know? Anyway, it's not the most important thing. I'm not going to marry for love. I'm going to marry for money. Just you wait and see!"

"But Martha, how could you marry someone you didn't love? Don't you want to be happy?"

"Of course I do! You just have to be careful who you choose, that's all. Look at Papa and Mama. Papa fell in love with the daughter of a river boat captain. Because she was pretty and danced like a feather. So now he lives in a pokey little house in Ipswich and teaches school. My brother Walter's got more sense. He's courting a girl with a bit of money."

"What's she like?"

"She's very pretty. And sweet. I just don't want her for a sister in law, that's all."

"Why not?"

Martha pulled a face. "Estelle Beauchamps thinks she's a cut above a little Ipswich girl like me. Just because her papa owns a property on the Downs." She bent down again and filled her hand with the scattered flowers. "Anyway Aunt Dot doesn't have a bad life. Uncle Eric's got some job in the government and spends a lot of time away from home. And she'll have the baby soon. If she wants somebody to love she can love it."

"When's it due?"

"Any day. So Grandmamma says." She laughed. "Wouldn't it be dreadful if it looked like *him?*" She turned to Sarah and tossed the handfuls of flowers up into the air so they landed on them both. "There! Don't we look wonderful?"

They didn't see Uncle Eric again. Another rain shower drove them back into the house where they found Mrs Greenaway anxious to be on the way home. She was expecting Walter on the train that afternoon and wanted to be at *Penzance* to greet him. Aunty Dot wasn't there either. She had gone upstairs to lie down and Grandmamma was in two minds whether to stay with her or go home. In the end she sent a servant to find Uncle Eric, who had gone off looking for things to shoot, and tell him to come back to the house straight away.

Half way home the rain came down suddenly in a grey curtain. The track turned into red mud. The creek was running high at the crossing as they splashed through, cold grey water pulling at the wheels of the carriage. They reached the house in time to see the wagonette from the station disappearing into the gloom along the track which led to the road. Standing on the verandah was a tall young man, dressed in city clothes, his wet hair slicked down to his scalp. At his feet, apart from a battered trunk and an

41

old cardboard suitcase, were Bertie and Jack and an assortment of dogs, all obviously delighted to see him.

Mrs. Greenaway let out a shriek of delight, the first unladylike thing Sarah had ever seen her do.

"Walter!"

Surrounded by the adoring throng, Walter went into the house. By the time he reached the drawing room the rest of the family had arrived. The noise was considerable, drowning out the sound of heavy rain drumming on the tin roof of the verandah outside the windows.

Walter stood in the middle of the room with his mother on one side and his grandmother on the other while the little boys fought for a place nearest to his feet. He shook his father and uncle by the hand. Answered questions about his journey. Greeted Angus with delight and asked him about school. Hugged Martha so hard that her feet left the ground. Kissed Anne's pale cheek. Strode across the room to meet Mrs Armitage, Grandmamma's housekeeper, who had brought the tea in herself. Took the tray off her and plonked it on the table, grabbed a hot scone from the top of the pile and crammed it into his mouth. Hugged the lady firmly, laughing around the crumbs.

Then it was Sarah's turn.

Mr Greenaway came across the room to where she had been standing on the fringe of the group. Took her by the hand and led her forward.

"This is Sarah." he said. "I told you about her."

Sarah looked up into Walter's eyes. They were dark like his father's. But there was nothing in them for her. No greeting. No warmth. Just cold dark depths like the water in the wash pool.

Walter reached up and carefully scooped his dark hair away from his face. Then he extended his hand.

"Pleased to meet you, Sarah," he said, not meaning a word of it.

And she knew she had an enemy.

4

David moved in as soon as he got back from Sydney and the only difference it made was that, instead of calling in every night or taking my mother out, he was there all the time. He was a good cook and fond of steak which he cooked rare with mushroom sauce and baked potatoes. It was worth having him around just for that.

A few weeks later we were sitting at the table after dinner, Mum working on her laptop while David and I discussed the rebuilding of the original homestead at *Penzance.* On a large piece of paper I drew a square and divided it into four smaller squares with a cross like a plus sign. "Four rooms, see? Living room, dining room, bedroom and nursery. That's all there was to it. Not even a kitchen. I wonder where they did the cooking?"

"No bathroom, either," said Mum from the other end of the table. "That's the part I couldn't handle."

"They usually had the kitchen separate," said David. "Then, if it caught fire, the rest of the house wouldn't burn down. And the bathroom was a jug of hot water, if you were lucky"

He reached for the pencil and began drawing elevations of the walls in that swift, sure way of his that was so interesting to watch.

"Shingle roof," he said. "Hessian walls probably."

"Hessian?"

"Like sacking. Whitewashed."

Silence for a while. Mum closed up her laptop with a click and got up to put the kettle on. "Have you found out why Walter dislikes Sarah so much?" She reached into the cupboard for mugs.

"Well, he doesn't believe what his father told him about her, for a start, or so Martha says. He thinks she's a gold digger. Out for what she can get."

"And what does she want to get?" This from David.

"*Penzance,* apparently."

"*Penzance?*" David lifted his head from his drawing. "But how?"

"By making Drew fall in love with her. Walter thinks she's flirting with him."

"What good will that do her?"

"Well, Drew's going to have *Penzance* one day."

Mum laughed. "I don't fancy her chances. From what I can see, Drew flirts with everyone. Including his cousin Martha."

"Yes, and Martha thinks she's got some sort of special relationship with Drew. *She* says Sarah's flirting with him just to make her jealous. But the point is Walter doesn't care who Drew likes or who Drew doesn't like. *His* attitude is that Sarah shouldn't be in a position to flirt with Drew. He says okay, his father's a soft touch. Everyone knows that. And maybe he's got a good reason for taking Sarah in. But she should be in the kitchen with Meggie, not living like one of the family."

"What's his problem, I wonder?" Mum put a pot of tea on the table.

"Well, my theory is that he fancies her," said David. "Like mad."

Mum laughed. "Fancies who? Sarah? You're just a hopeless romantic, David. Admit it!"

David grinned at me. "Time will tell!"

I had my cup of tea and went up to bed, leaving the love-birds to do the washing up. I took the old diary with me, keen to read on.

It was not only the situation between Sarah and Walter that intrigued me. There was also the question of Sarah's relationship with the Greenaways. Who was she? Where had she come from? That was one thing I was no nearer to finding out.

It was a warm night and I lay on top of my sheets, the ceiling fan turning slowly above my head. I opened the old book carefully and peered at the faded writing.

"With the family all together for the first time, dinner that night was a special affair. Everyone was expected to dress up,

Martha and me included. We even had Meggie to help us get dressed. Penzance *has a whole population of servants to do the cleaning, the washing, the cooking and the waiting on tables so, while we are here, all Meggie has to do is look after Ethel and act as lady's maid to Martha's mother and to us."*

Meggie had their best clothes laid out on the bed. Sarah's green striped muslin that Martha had pinched off Lizzie Sangster and Martha's white with a pattern of tiny red flowers.

While she combed their hair, Meggie talked non-stop about all the wonders of *Penzance.* About Mrs Armitage who was really nice once you got to know her and her husband who was in charge of the stables and drove the big coach on special occasions. About the other girls and the romps they got up to. About little Mary who washed the dishes and cried every night into the dish water because she wanted to go home.

About a certain under-gardener called Rory O'Neil who came into the kitchen in the afternoons to have his tea. He had the biggest brownest eyes she'd ever seen and all the girls said he was keen on her, nothing surer, because he'd been outside the kitchen door when Ellen went out to empty the tea leaves onto the garden and he'd asked for her name.

By the time all that had been said, Martha's hair had been brushed, polished with a silk handkerchief and fastened up with a ribbon and Sarah's had been brushed, despaired over and tied back with an alice band, their dresses tweaked and straightened and Martha's gold chain fastened around her neck.

Sarah had nothing to wear but Meggie solved the problem by fetching a length of black velvet ribbon and sewing onto it a pretty gold filigree button with a pearl in the middle.

"This is what us girls do that don't have no gold necklaces to wear," Maggie said, her head bent low over her work.

Fastened around Sarah's neck, it made her skin glow and added a sparkle to her eyes. It also made Martha jealous, although she was hardly likely to say so seeing as Sarah was wearing a bit of home made rubbish made by the servant. Which rather took the edge off their arrival at their first grown-up dinner party.

The table in the dining room was set for ten. Dominated by the big silver candlesticks, and decorated with green leaves from the garden, it had a festive air, the soft candlelight gleaming on silver cutlery, crystal glasses and gold-ribbed plates.

Used to the gaslight in Ipswich, Sarah was yet to become accustomed to the gloom of candlelit rooms and the feeling of having the darkness at her back, just out of reach. And it was very dark at *Penzance* with nothing outside the windows except the hot night sky and the reflection of a new moon gleaming on thick clouds.

They found their places. Grandmamma and Uncle John at each end of the table and the rest arranged down each side. On one side, Martha's papa next to Grandmamma, then Sarah, then Angus, then Mama. On the other side, Drew next to Grandmamma, then Martha, then Walter then Anne. Which gave Sarah Papa and Angus either side and Walter almost opposite, staring at her through the greenery with unfriendly eyes.

In between mouthfuls of food the Greenaways talked. Papa to Grandmamma. Mama to Uncle John. Uncle John the full length of the table to question Papa. It seemed that Papa had come to *Penzance* with the intention of pursuing a recent interest in photography, an interest for which he had neither the time nor the space in Ipswich. He was keen to have the use of one of the farm sheds but Grandmamma was of the opinion that he would probably blow himself up and half the property with him.

Drew and Martha spoke exclusively to each other except when Grandmamma directed a remark in their direction. Martha was flirting, tossing her hair and looking at Drew from under lowered lashes. Drew was enjoying it. It seemed to be a game they had played before but there was no denying the look of admiration in Drew's eyes. There was no denying either that Martha was looking as attractive as a fifteen year old girl could look who was not allowed to put up her hair or wear the low-necked gowns that the older women were wearing to show off necks and throats that were no longer their best feature.

Anne, looking pale and unwell, picked at her food, saying nothing, while her eyes darted around the table. Every now and then Walter turned from his conversation and spoke earnestly to her, trying to persuade her to eat.

Each time Anne made a little show of giving in to him which, Sarah thought, would have been charming, if anybody else had been doing it. But there was nothing charming about Anne Greenaway with her limp yellow hair, her sallow skin and those knowing, disapproving, unfriendly eyes.

By contrast, Walter was all dark good looks. His high, starched collar accentuated his narrow features and dark eyes. His hair was thick and wavy, springing from a peak which defied all attempts to flatten it down, and long enough to touch the collar of his jacket. Sarah watched him place his slender, long-fingered hand on Anne's arm and imagined the warmth of it against her skin.

He's by far the best looking boy at the table, she thought. It's just a pity his nature's as sour as that of his cousin. They make a fine pair! She dismissed them from her thoughts and turned to Angus.

He hadn't spoken all evening except to tell Grandmamma that, yes, thank you, he was quite comfortable and Uncle John that, no, he didn't want any more meat.

"How do you like *Penzance*?" she asked. "It must be nice to be away from city life and back in the country again."

He turned his head, chewing steadily and said nothing.

She tried again. "Is this what it's like in your own country?"

He shook his head. "No. Smaller."

"What d'you mean, smaller?"

"See that paddock in front of the house?" He nodded with his head. "If you set off in the morning to ride around our front paddock at home, you wouldn't be back for three days."

"Why's that? Slow horses?"

He grinned. "No, not slow horses. It's just that it's a very big paddock. Not like here where everything's divided up. Neighbours all around. I've never even been to the edge of our place. If you want to see what we own, you have to look on a map."

"It's cattle country up there, isn't it?"

"Yeah, cattle country. Channel country, we're in. Plenty of water. Rich country. The grass just grows and grows."

Sarah smiled. "You're not a poet, are you, Angus?"

"I leave that to the other blokes. They say it better than I can."

"Banjo Patterson. Do you know him?

Clancy's gone to Queensland droving, and we don't know where he are."

"I know that one." Angus was staring into the candle flames.

"In my wild erratic fancy visions come to me of Clancy, gone a-droving down the Cooper where the Western drovers go.

What's that bit in the middle? About the bush?"

Sarah quoted softly,

"And the bush has friends to meet him, and their kindly voices greet him
In the murmur of the breezes and the river on its bars.
And he sees the vision splendid of the sunlit plains extended,
and at night the wondrous glory of the everlasting stars."

Lying on my bed under the slowly turning fan sudden tears sting my eyes, blurring the words on the page. Because I know that poem. My father taught it to me. He's no poet, my dad, any more than Angus was. He's a television producer and he'd wanted to turn *Clancy of the Overflow* into a mini series.

He had a tape of the poem in the car which he used to play on his way into endless meetings about money and sponsorship, psyching himself into the mood. I remember him going along the highway with his fingers tapping impatiently on the sheepskin covered steering wheel and his eyes on the distant towers of the city, quoting the last verse.

"And I somehow rather fancy that I'd like to change with Clancy,
Like to take a turn at droving where the seasons come and go."

And I used to think 'as if' because my father was a city man through and through. I don't think he'd ever been outside Melbourne's boundaries in his life unless he was on a plane and then it was only to swap one city for another.

But Dad was in Melbourne and it was David I could hear downstairs, laughing with Mum. And it didn't really matter how many times I told my mother, or tried to convince myself, that I didn't mind the way things were, the truth was I missed him. Then suddenly, in the midst of my misery, I found myself thinking about Greg Hall, stuck in Toowoomba with his mad little mother, and wondered whether he ever lay on his bed and cried for his dad, too.

Of course *Penzance* didn't open for Christmas. There were delays and delays, a great many of which were created by David allowing his imagination to run away with him. David's imagination caused the building of an outdoor eating area between the big house and the old house and a natural instinct for comfort on Allie's part, together with stories told by the locals about the ferocity of Downs winters, meant that it had to be roofed and a fireplace built in.

I hadn't been up there since the first visit and, steeped as I was in the events of Sarah's diary, I could imagine *Penzance* only as it had been that Christmas in 1892. Horror stories of plumbing disasters and long discussions about the number of diners Allie would be able to seat in comfort seemed to be about some other place.

After New Year, Mum, David and I went to Byron Bay for two weeks, staying in a cottage owned by a friend of David's. It was situated on a secluded beach some distance from town, hidden in banksia scrub and separated from the beach by a low hump of dry sand. Mum was sick of *Penzance* by this time and I think she hoped that David and I would leave it all behind us in Ipswich and settle down to a lazy family holiday. But I brought the lap-top and the diary and David brought the mobile phone.

The days settled into a pattern. Early mornings, while David and Mum lay in bed, I went along the beach. Five o'clock on a hot summer morning is not too early for surfers, or for dolphins either, and I would sit and watch them riding the waves, the boys' voices coming to me, thin and far away. Sometimes I would see an eagle motionless in the pale sky, or swooping the length of the beach. Then I would swim. Diving under the breaking waves, I would pace up and down the beach, feeling my muscles remember their training and glorying in that long smooth action that had almost got me into the zone squad. But this was pure pleasure.

Then back to the house to find Mum and David awake and David gone to town on the ancient bicycle he'd found in the shed to buy milk and papers, and fresh bread or croissants. And, by the time we had finished eating breakfast, it would be too hot to do anything else and I would get out the lap-top and set myself up in my favourite place in the corner of the wide deck with a gnarled banksia tree overhead. And David would go and hide somewhere and make his phone calls. To Allie. To the builder. To the person who was doing the stained glass for the little round window at home, which was Mum's Christmas present.

Half way through the second week Mum rebelled. She locked the lap-top in the linen cupboard and threatened to confiscate David's phone if she saw him on it again. But by then the stained-glass window had been installed and all that remained was for us to delay our journey home the following Saturday so that we would arrive in the afternoon when the sunlight would be streaming through it, just as I had imagined.

And I was almost finished. There were only a few pages left in the diary. Before I handed the computer over to Mum, I printed out an extra copy of what I had done, stuck it in an envelope and rode the bicycle into town to post it to Greg.

"24th December 1892

It's hard to believe it's Christmas already! The last week has gone so fast. Angus has been teaching me to ride and I've been out every day. Apart from being too sore to sit down (and too tired to write my diary!), it's been really good.

There were several advantages to the riding lessons which Sarah received every day during that week leading up to Christmas. The first was being taught by one of the best riders in Queensland.

Angus rode with the strange loose-limbed, hunch-backed stockman's style that allowed him to stay in the saddle all day. This is what he taught Sarah to do and, while he was doing so, they ranged all over the country around *Penzance,* exploring creeks and forests and great paddocks full of grass trees, standing shoulder to shoulder as far as the misty hills.

The second advantage was that Sarah was away from the house for most of the day which meant that she only had to put up with Walter glaring at her during dinner and, even then, not always because sometimes the Greenaways had visitors and then the two girls had nursery tea with the little boys while the grown-ups, including Walter, Drew and Angus, dined in style. It also gave Martha free rein to flirt with Drew as much as she liked which kept her in good temper, always a good idea when Sarah had to share a bed with her.

Once she got past his shyness, Sarah found Angus was a kind, gentle, funny boy. He was one of the only people she'd met who took her as he found her and wasn't interested in poking and prying into her past. Coming as he did from an isolated cattle station in the north of Queensland, he was as much a misfit in Darling Downs society as Sarah was and, when confronted by the huge gaps in her knowledge or the peculiar things that she did know, he put it all down to her being a Melbourne girl.

To him, Melbourne was the great unknown, a place of such strangeness that he was at a loss to imagine what it was like and he often questioned Sarah about it. Angus was going to Melbourne after the summer to do a law course and he wasn't looking forward to it. After all, if he found the Downs small and restricting, what was he going to do with himself in a big city?

What Sarah didn't know was that riding with Angus was causing a great deal of interest and speculation amongst the rest of the family. Coming home each afternoon to the approval of Grandmamma and Papa, she simply assumed they were pleased she was enjoying herself. It never occurred to her they were rubbing their hands with glee because she had managed to catch for herself a member of one of the richest grazing families in the colony.

Christmas Day was grey and humid. With dawn not long after four o'clock and small children in the house, the day started early to the sound of Bertie and Jack galloping excitedly up and down the stairs, followed by the roar of Uncle John's voice telling them not to do it.

Church was at ten o'clock. Sarah and Martha travelled in the back of Grandmamma's buggy, squashed in with Anne and the two little boys, while Mama and Grandmamma sat up front wearing their newly-trimmed hats. Bertie and Jack had found sugar mice in the toes of their stockings and, as soon as Mama and Grandmamma had their backs turned, the mice appeared from their pockets, sticky and covered with fluff and were shoved into their mouths, noses first so that the string tails hung out.

"Bertie, that is revolting!" said Martha in a carrying voice. "If you put your sticky fingers *anywhere near* my new frock, you can get out and walk!"

They returned to Christmas dinner, served in the dining room with the doors wide open to admit whatever damp breeze happened to be passing. The turkey, which had been alive two days ago and whose long tail feathers had gone to adorn the ladies' hats, sat in the middle of the table, full of rich bread stuffing and surrounded by dishes of steaming vegetables. Bertie and Jack were at the table, subdued by dire warnings if they didn't behave, and little Ethel with a tea towel swathed around her neck to save her new print frock. She insisted in eating her dinner standing up, singing *Baa baa black sheep* between mouthfuls and scraping her little button boots on Grandmamma's best balloon-backed chairs.

Later on Papa said he wanted to take a family photograph in the garden so everyone trooped out onto the lawn where chairs had been set up under the shade of a big tree. The ground was soft and broken up with tree roots and the little boys managed to fall over and get the backs of their best pants dirty. Grandmamma sat in the middle with Ethel on her knee. Mama and Anne sat either side with Sarah and Martha behind and the boys and men filling up the gaps on either side. Martha complained about Anne sitting while she and Sarah had to stand but Papa said he needed to balance out the picture and Grandmamma said, somewhat sternly, that Anne was too poorly to stand up in the heat and that Martha should be thankful she had her health. Which made Martha roll her eyes up in her head, just as Papa pressed the shutter, and spoil the picture.

"And I'll get the blame for it, too, you'll see," Martha grumbled later as they lay together in bed. "It's not fair! Anne always gets her own way, just because she's sick. And Walter sticks up for her all the time. They're as thick as thieves, those two. Always looking for things to criticise. I don't know why they don't just leave me alone!" Martha humped herself over onto her side.

"It's not just you, Mattie. They don't like me much either, especially Walter."

"I don't know why you let him bother you, Sarah." Martha's voice was muffled by the pillow. "Walter's just like that with some people. He either likes them or he doesn't. There isn't anything you can do about it. Everybody else thinks you're just fine, *one* person in particular."

One person?

"Who, Mattie?"

But Martha had drifted into sleep.

On Boxing Day most of the family took off after breakfast to go to the Races at Drayton. Drew told Angus that it was the greatest fun with everyone on horseback and races going on all the time. Angus wanted Sarah to go. He said it would be a good opportunity for her to show off what she had learned. But Sarah had her own plans. When the Drayton party had finally sorted themselves out and galloped away, there was nobody left in the house but the servants, Ethel, who was too little to go, Anne, who was too sick and had stayed in bed, and Martha who said she had better things to do than ride around on horses all day in the heat and had stayed behind to practice her piano piece one last time before the grand concert.

This concert was the high point of Christmas at *Penzance* and everyone had to do something, even the totally untalented like Sarah and Angus. They had been taking Angus' battered copy of Banjo Patterson out with them each day with the idea that they would be able to recite some poetry. It sounded perfectly fine on horseback out in the middle of the bush but Sarah hoped Angus would have the nerve to stand up in front of an audience that didn't consist of just her and a couple of horses.

But all that was for later. In the meantime, like Martha, Sarah had better things to do. She was going swimming. She had already taken an old sheet from the linen cupboard to dry herself and, with this tucked under her arm, she escaped the house and ran down the slope towards the creek. By the time she reached the trees at the bottom of the slope she could feel the sharp sting of the sun on her arms and the sweat sliding down the skin on her back.

She plunged into the trees and followed the track that led to the wash pool. It lay dark and mysterious under the shifting canopy of the trees, full to the brim with dark, still water that reflected the leaves fluttering in the warm breeze. She looked around carefully. There was nobody there. A kookaburra landed on a branch above her head and peered down at her with its head on one side. He tipped back his head and laughed.

Sarah took off her clothes as quickly as she could and left them on a rock in a neatly folded pile. She made a curious sight in her lace-trimmed camisole and frilly drawers, standing at one end of the wash pool, poised for her dive. But then the water folded over her head, cool and delicious. It felt like silk on her water-starved body. She opened her eyes and saw the sun striking golden shafts through the murky water, lighting up the black muck on the bottom.

She did ten laps without stopping, feeling the pull of muscles which had done no work for months. Then with her legs and arms shaking with exertion, she floated for a while, watching the clouds ride across the gaps in the leaves. The fresh morning was gone. She could feel the humidity in the air and the patter of rain on the leaves as a shower passed over. Not that she cared. It could rain all it liked. She was wet already.

She was back in the pool with her head down counting what was to be her last ten laps when Drew walked into the clearing. She came to a halt at his feet and looked up into his face

"Drew! What are you doing here?"

"I was just about to ask you the same question."

"Are you by yourself?"

"I am at the moment. What have you got *on*?"

"Never mind that. Be serious, Drew!"

"The others are on their way. I rode ahead."

She looked around frantically. Her clothes and the old sheet were at the other end of the pool.

"There's an old sheet up there. Get it for me, will you, Drew? I've got to go."

"I'll say you have," said Drew good-humouredly as he ambled along the edge of the pool. "There'll be hell to pay if they find you here."

"Hurry up then, will you?" She was beginning to shiver. "How far ahead were you anyway?"

"Far enough."

Drew came back and held out the sheet.

"You say. Angus can outride you any day and you know it. They'll probably be here any second. Open it up, can't you?"

He did so.

"And turn your head."

Sarah climbed out of the water, wrapped herself in the sheet and stood shivering and dripping water onto the ground.

"Now what are you going to do?" Drew was watching her with admiration.

"I'm off home. I'll be back before you, if I hurry. And don't you tell ..."

But it was too late. Cheerful voices, feet running and the clearing was full of people. Bertie and Jack first, already stripping off their clothes and pushing each other to be first in. Then they saw Sarah, wet and shivering, wrapped in a bedraggled bedsheet, standing at the far end of the pool with Drew behind her, his hands still resting on her shoulders where they had been since he wrapped the sheet around her not ten seconds previously.

Silence.

Across the black water rows of eyes. Bertie and Jack subdued and bashful with their shirts off and their singlets showing. Papa and Uncle John, their faces stern. Angus with a look on his face that said 'betrayal!' though all Sarah had been doing was having a swim.

Uncle John recovered first. He strode towards them. "What the devil is going on here?"

Sarah fell Drew's hands drop from her shoulders. She stared into Uncle John's angry face.

"I was only having a swim! I didn't think I was doing anything wrong."

"Only having a swim? A swim?" John Greenaway stood in front of Sarah. Thrust his face into hers, "Young ladies don't swim. Or, at least, here they don't. Nice young ladies around here don't take their clothes off and disport themselves in muddy puddles. Especially not with a boy around."

He turned to his son.

"Have you been in, too? Or were you just watching?"

"Neither, Father. I found her swimming and helped her out. That's all. I didn't know she was going to be here."

"The pity of it is, don't believe you! Look, Drew, you can go to the devil for all I care. Just take yourself off somewhere else and do it, d'you mind? And don't expect any support from me!" And then, to Sarah, "Now I'll take you home."

The rain came down as they left the shelter of the trees, Sarah and Uncle John in front with Drew following and the rest of them in a bunch at the back.

Sarah walked up the slope back to the house on wildly shuddering legs with the sodden sheet around her shoulders, John Greenaway's hand cruel in the small of her back and the cold grey rain falling all around.

The rest of the family must have seen them coming because they were crowded in the hall when they went in. Grandmamma with her hands clasped on her bosom, Mama with her face drained of colour, Martha staring angrily from Sarah to Drew and back again and Anne on the stairs in her nightgown crying out in a thin voice that she had always known Sarah was up to no good ever since she first arrived and why did nobody ever listen to her?

Walter, who hadn't been at the wash pool, came into the hall, freshly washed and combed, just as Sarah arrived at the bottom of the stairs, wrapped in her muddy sheet. He stopped, scooping his damp hair away from his forehead, and Sarah could feel his hatred flow across the space between them so that it seemed as if there was nobody else there.

Then Grandmamma came forward. "I'll take you to your room," she said, putting her arm across Sarah's shoulders. She stared around. "The rest of you, go and have your tea."

She led Sarah away. The family, released from the tension of the moment, began to drift towards the tea table talking amongst themselves. Bits of conversation floated back to Sarah as she puddled across the cool floor in the direction of her room. Mama talking soothingly to Anne as she led her back up the stairs. Bertie telling Jack that he'd seen Sarah and Drew kissing just before everyone arrived in the clearing and Jack saying it was nothing new, Drew kissed everybody. Papa telling his brother that we were behind the times in Queensland. "Swimming's all the rage down south, so I'm told. Very beneficial to the health." Martha hissing at Drew, "I might have known you'd be involved." and Drew's reply, "But she can swim, Mattie! You should have seen her. I've never seen anything like it."

And, just as Sarah reached the door, there was Walter, his face white with rage. "You hussy! I knew it all along. But I never thought you'd go this far!"

He reached out to grab her but Grandmamma put her hand in Sarah's back and shoved her through the door. She turned around. "Don't be foolish, boy." she said sharply. "It's all been a silly misunderstanding. Nothing more than that. Now go and have your tea before it stews."

After breakfast the following day Sarah was summoned to Grandmamma's parlour where she found her sitting at the desk, busy with some papers.

"Sit down, child." Grandmamma turned around on her chair and looked at Sarah for a long moment. "I fixed things up, did you know that? There won't be any more trouble."

Sarah stared up at the old woman. "Am I supposed to thank you? Because I don't think I did anything wrong."

"Whether you think it was wrong or not, going swimming in your drawers was hardly the most sensible thing to do, was it, Sarah? Especially with a boy there."

"But Drew wasn't there! He only just arrived ahead of the others."

"Ah, yes. And here is the difficulty. When you two were found together apparently embracing by the wash pool, Drew had already been missing from the Races for several hours. It was assumed, it now appears wrongly, that you and he had been together all afternoon. It wouldn't be the first time Drew has been involved in that sort of caper."

"Where was he then? If he wasn't with me."

"He hasn't said. Won't say. Only that he wasn't with you."

"Saving my skin? Or his own?"

Grandmamma shrugged. "A bit of both, I daresay." She leaned forward. "Anyway, there's no harm done. Not so far as you are concerned at any rate."

"Except for Martha. She thinks there's something going on between me and Drew. What is it with her anyway? She treats him like her own private property."

"Martha has adored Drew ever since she was a tiny girl. Followed him everywhere when she was little. Of course, Drew didn't mind. He loves attention, as you have probably noticed. And I didn't see what harm it could do. He lost his mother when he was only a little chap. It's a bit different, now they are older."

"Do you think they'll get married?"

Grandmamma hooted with laughter.

"Martha and Drew? I shouldn't think so. They're far too much alike."

"Cousins, you mean?"

"No, no. Not that. Although cousins do marry, even in these modern times. I mean they're too self-centred. The pair of them. They wouldn't last five minutes!" She turned around to her desk and began shuffling the papers into a pile. "In one way, I'm glad this happened. It's made me see things more clearly. I'm going to send Drew to boarding school next year to knock some of the nonsense out of him before it's too late. Perhaps not Ipswich though. Not with Martha making cow-eyes at him from across the street." It was almost as if she was talking to herself. "He can go to Sydney. Far enough away for him to make his own mistakes and no Grandmamma to pull him out of the mess. And Walter's down there. He'll keep an eye on him."

Sarah opened her mouth to speak but Grandmamma beat her to it.

"I know you don't like him."

"It's him that doesn't like me! You saw the way he spoke to me last night!"

Grandmamma leaned back in her chair. "I've spoken to Walter. Told him there was nothing whatsoever happening between you and Drew. How could there be when it's as plain as day you're walking out with Angus Buchanan?"

"Doing *what* with Angus?"

"Walking out with him. I mean, you do ride together every day. Which is a fair indication of which way the wind's blowing. Even in this day and age."

"Does Angus know this? That we're ... walking out together?"

"He's very fond of you, Sarah."

"Fond of me? What's that supposed to mean?"

"Well, that's for him to decide, of course. But he's a good catch, Sarah. You could do a lot worse!"

"A good *catch?* But I'm only fifteen! Why can't people leave me alone?"

Grandmamma turned around and laid her hand gently on Sarah's knee. "If you want them to do that, you'll have to give them the opportunity. Perhaps you ought to steer clear of the boys for a little while, eh? I have to sort the linen next week. How about you lend me a hand?"

5

Penzance had changed almost beyond recognition. New roof, new windows, raw timber on the floor of the verandah, half-painted iron lace railings. The house was hung with painters' scaffolding and had the abandoned look of all such places when the workmen are not around.

Greg was standing at the top of the steps and came down to the footpath to greet us. He was taller than I remembered, his eyes looking darker than ever in a tanned face. He loped ahead of us up the steps and opened the door. From inside came the sound of music, very loud, and someone singing off-key.

"Ma!" he yelled. "They're here."

The music stopped abruptly and Allie came out of some back room, bustling and jangling, bringing with her the smell of fresh-brewed coffee.

"My dears, you're just in time!" Kisses all round. "Kirsty, you look marvellous! Doesn't she look marvellous, Greg?"

The hall was draped with paint-splattered dust cloths, the floor protected by sheets of cardboard. Allie hustled us into a back room, furnished with plastic garden furniture and over-flowing cardboard boxes. A table by the window held coffee cups and a fruit cake which smelled as if it had just come out of the oven.

"I thought we'd have coffee in here. We're going to have a picnic lunch. I thought you might like that better." Allie wrinkled up her nose. "The house smells too much of paint."

She poured the coffee and handed the cups around.

"I'm going to have this room for myself. What d'you think?"

"It's a nice little room." Mum took her coffee cup. "Are you going to use it as an office?"

"Goodness, no! Nothing like that. I always do the accounts in the kitchen. I just thought it would be somewhere to sit quietly away from the customers, always supposing I have any. Allie's parlour, isn't that what they would have called it in the old days?"

Well, it had been Grandmamma's parlour, too, a pretty room which had looked out into the gloom of the back yard dominated by the ancient bunya pine. But now the tree had gone, the old kitchen had gone and the view was of a newly-planted garden and a patchwork lawn sloping to a view of brown pasture and the smudge of hills on the horizon.

"How are you getting on with your solicitor, Allie?" asked David, accepting a re-fill of his cup and reaching for a second slice of cake.

Allie snorted. "Mr Brownlow? I don't know how Lottie put up with him. I don't think the old fool likes dealing with women. Sometimes I think he forgets who'll be paying his bill."

"Has he told you how long it'll be before everything is finalised?"

"He says I'll have probate by the end of next week. Then the deeds can go in to have the name changed."

"What about the liquor licence?"

"I'm going to sort that out myself. It's something I used to look after down in Sydney so I know how to go about it. And the Health Inspector's been organised. Don't *fret*, David!" Allie reached out her hand for Mum's cup. "Actually, I wondered if Kirsty would like to come into Brisbane with us some time next week. I've got paper work to attend to but I'm sure Greg would enjoy her company."

"Sounds like a great idea," said Mum. "What do you think, Kirsty?"

I looked up and caught Greg's eye. He was looking pleased and hopeful.

"Yeah, okay. I suppose it'd be all right."

Greg's dark hair had fallen across his forehead and I watched him scoop it up with one hand in a gesture that was infinitely familiar and made me feel acutely uncomfortable. The trouble with Greg was that he reminded me of somebody but I didn't know who. I didn't even know if the person he reminded me of was someone I liked or someone I didn't like. All I knew was that, when I was with him, all I wanted to do was get away and, when I was away, I cursed myself for missing my chance.

"Well, that's organised!" Allie got to her feet. "Now, if you'll excuse me, I've got things to do in the kitchen."

Greg rolled his eyes. "A picnic, she says. The only part of it that'll be like a picnic is eating it outdoors!"

David laughed. "I'm not complaining! Don't forget, I've eaten your mum's cooking. Now, come on Kirsty. I want to show you the new building."

The pile of rubble was long gone, replaced by a low, square building with a shingle roof pulled down like an old hat. Wide paved verandahs ran all around, edged with wooden railings.

We went in through a sliding window. "They're going to be motel-style units," said David. "A bit cheaper than staying in the house. But nice." He walked across the concrete floor and pulled open a sliding door. "Bathroom here, see? And there'll be a little kitchen along that wall. What d'you think?"

I walked out of the room and leaned my arms on the verandah railing, staring across at the houses on the other side of the street.

"This used to be the front paddock," I said. "There were always horses in here. It was green, too, that year because of the rain. Not like now." I indicated the hot sky.

David leaned next to me. "Where was the road to town?"

I pointed. "It went across the bottom of the paddock . Beyond where those houses are now."

"That's where the main road is now. That's probably why it has that big kink in it, because it used to go around the Greenaway's paddock." He grinned. "I have a friend in town planning and they drive him nuts, country roads. If he had his way he'd bulldoze the lot and start again."

We turned around and stared at the building.

"It's as close to authentic as I could make it," said David. "I got hold of some old photographs so I know what it used to look like. I thought I'd frame some of them and put them in the rooms. What d'you think?"

Greg appeared at the entrance to the covered dining area which linked the house with the new building. "Lunch is ready." He led the way. "We're having it here. Mum says it's too hot outside."

"Some picnic," I said.

He grinned.

As promised, the food was delicious. A bacon and egg pie in crisp, home-made pastry, stir- fried potatoes rich with garlic and coriander and a rice salad like I'd never seen before, full of fresh tomatoes and chunks of ham. When we had finished Allie placed a cold fruit platter in the middle of the table.

"How are you getting on with the dreaded Walter?" Allie asked me, peeling a peach and popping the slices one by one into her mouth. "Is he still being a beast?"

"Ah, well, we've got a theory about Walter," said David, leaning back in his chair

"A theory?" I said. "You haven't told me!"

He glanced at Mum. "We only thought of it last night. But it's a good one! Answers a lot of questions."

"David reckons Sarah is Mr Greenaway's daughter," said Mum. She picked up her glass and sipped her wine. "I knew you'd be surprised! So was I when he first mentioned it."

"Think about it," said David, leaning forward. "It explains where she came from. *And* why Walter hates her so much."

"If he *knew,* you mean?" said Allie. "Or guessed? What do you think, Kirsty?"

I pulled a face. "Mr Greenaway's *daughter*? What, you mean he had a girl-friend or something? They didn't do that sort of thing in those days, did they?"

"I'm sure they did," said David. "I don't think human nature has changed that much."

"Well, d'you reckon he *knew* about her? Or did she just turn up on the doorstep one day?"

"Perhaps she did. Not literally on the doorstep. But he would've had to take her in - his own daughter. What choice would he have?"

"And Mrs Greenaway?"

"Maybe the story about Mr Greenaway's friend in Melbourne was all she knew."

"But Walter knew the truth? Is that what you're saying?"

"Or doesn't believe the lie. Whichever way it goes, he obviously doesn't like the idea of Sarah being part of the family."

"Well, you can see his point of view," said Mum. "Mr Greenaway was already raising four kids. And sending Walter to university wouldn't be cheap."

"So what did you do in a situation like that?" asked Allie. "I'm talking about Sarah's mother now. It must have been very difficult for her. Being a single mother was hard enough thirty years ago, never mind in Victorian times."

"Being a single mother would have been *impossible* in Victorian times," said David. "She'd have had to move away. Find work to support them both. Dress-making or millinery or something like that."

"What's *millinery*?" asked Greg.

"Making hats. Ladies were very fond of their hats in those days. Feathers, lace, ribbons, the lot!"

"It all sounds dreadfully Dickensian," said Allie

"Well, it would have been. There was no social security in those days, remember. Survival was a very chancy thing."

"And then what?" I asked. "I mean how come Sarah ended up with the Greenaways?"

"Who knows? Maybe her mum died."

"So much for your idea that Sarah and Walter were going to end up loving each other. According to you, they were brother and sister!"

David shrugged. "Well, it's only a theory. You're welcome to shoot it down in flames, if you want to."

"No, I think you could be right. It does explain a few things. Like that ... I don't know what you'd call it. A sense ... a feeling of disapproval. All the time. And not just from Walter and Anne who just plain hate her!" I shrugged. "It's difficult to explain. And, have you noticed? She doesn't seem to be able to *do* anything. She can't play the piano. Can't sew. Can't recite poetry. I mean, where's she *been?*"

"Her mother probably didn't have the time to teach her those things, if she was busy earning a living," said Mum.

"She seems a bit like me sometimes."

"Don't be silly, Kirsty!" said Mum a little too quickly. "How can you say such a thing? *You* have a family that loves you."

"I'll make us some coffee." Allie stood up and began clearing the table. She turned to Greg. "Are you going to take Kirsty down to the creek?'

Greg turned to me. "Do you want to? I thought we might go and look for this washpool of yours."

Together we walked down the long slope of the street until we came to the bridge. Ducking under the railings, we slithered down to where the water lay, a sullen trickle almost hidden by long grass.

"I've been down here a few times since I got your letter," said Greg. "You'd think there'd be something left. But I can't find a thing."

"It'd be further along."

We walked in single file. Mosquitoes stung our arms and legs. A smell of something slimy and rotten filled our nostrils. On both sides, back fences hemmed us in. Here and there mounds of grass clippings and garden rubbish were piled against the fences. After a while we left the houses behind and, a moment later, came out of the trees into the intense heat of the afternoon.

Greg pointed. "Look, you can see the house."

I tipped back my head. The old house wallowed in the afternoon sun, the light glinting from its windows. "We've come too far. You couldn't see *Penzance* from where the pool was."

Greg sat down in the dry grass. "Well, it's not here then. I've already looked back there."

I flopped down next to him. "A hundred years is a long time, you know, Greg. And the wash pool was derelict even then. Hadn't been used for twenty years."

"Wasn't that weird, that stuff about Sarah going swimming? What d'you reckon? She was extra-modern or they were extra old-fashioned?"

"A bit of both, I think. But I don't think it was the swimming that caused the trouble. It was the fact that Drew was there."

"So what was their problem? *Walter's* problem? What did he think she'd *done?*"

"Been in a compromising position with Drew. At least, that's what Grandmamma said. *She* said that in the olden days - that is, longer ago than eighteen ninety two - a girl could lose her reputation for doing something like that. And the boy could be forced to marry her. I suppose Walter thought it was part of Sarah's scheme to get her hands on *Penzance.*"

"What do you think, Kirsty? Do you think Sarah was after *Penzance?* And Drew?"

"I shouldn't think so. Sarah didn't even like him!"

Greg leaned forward. "And what about you and me? Am I going to have any better luck than Drew?"

"What do you mean?"

"Oh, come on, Kirsty! What's your problem? I don't usually have this much trouble getting a girl to like me!"

I glanced at him. "Then why bother?"

"Why *bother?* You're something special, Kirsty. I knew it the first time we met. It's just a pity the feeling isn't mutual."

I looked up to where the old house glinted in the sunlight. Remembered standing with Greg in that ruined bedroom. The quick sizzle of attraction between us. The way Greg devoured me with those dark eyes of his. Like he was doing now. In the grass his hand was very close to mine.

I pulled away. "I'm sorry, Greg."

"Oh, I get it. I'm sorry, Greg, I really *like* you." An imitation of a girl's voice. "You'll be telling me I'm nice next."

"Well, you are."

"Yes but what does it mean? You're a great bloke but push off because I've got my eye on someone else?" He leaned forward. *"Is* there someone else, Kirsty?"

I shook my head.

"Except for the Greenaways, eh? Sometimes I think you care more for them than you do for real people!"

"You're interested in them, too!"

Greg pulled a face. "To be honest, I've never been all that interested in the Greenaways, Kirsty. They were really only an excuse to get close to you."

"How d'you mean?"

"They gave me a reason to get Mum to invite you up to *Penzance*. Gave me an excuse to ring you up from time to time. Why else would I be interested in a bunch of dead people?" He laughed. "The oldies think we're really cute, you know that? Getting excited over an old diary. Little did they know what was really on my mind."

"Greg, I ..."

"And don't say 'sorry' again! Being rejected by the girl of my dreams is just something I've got to get used to."

I grinned.

"You're full of shit, Greg Hall, you know that?"

He grinned back.

"Come on, Kirsty, let's get back. It's hot out here."

He held out his hand and pulled me to my feet.

We began to climb the long slope of the hill towards the house.

And then, "Kirsty ... ?" Greg stopped walking. "What d'you think happened to Sarah?"

I shook my head. "I have no idea. Why d'you wanna know?"

"It doesn't matter. It's just that ... Have you ever thought that Sarah might be Lottie's mother?"

"Lottie's *mother*? How d'you work that one out?"

"Listen, I've been thinking about it. Lottie owned *Penzance*, right? Then she passed it on to Dad. So who did she get it from? She must have been related, that's what I reckon. To the Greenaways in the diary. So if Sarah married one of them ..."

"... like Drew for example?"

"Well, maybe. The thing is, it's one way we could find out what happened to Sarah."

"And what if she isn't Lottie's mother?"

I started walking again. It was fiercely hot.

"Come on, Kirsty! It's worth a try, isn't it? We've got the house, the Greenaways, Sarah's diary. If we could link them all together ..."

"It'd link you to Sarah. I supposed you'd like that."

"How d'you mean?"

"Think about it, dummy! If Sarah married a Greenaway and had Lottie. And Lottie's your – what? Great grandmother? Then you and Sarah would be related."

Greg's eyes blazed with enthusiasm. "That's cool!"

I tried to push down the worm of jealousy that crawled in my brain. I mean, it was *my* diary, right? Sometimes I think people forgot that.

Greg held open the kitchen door. Cold air reached out.

"Your dad's in television, isn't he? Your real dad, I mean. "

"He's a producer. Freelance. Why?"

"You ought to tell *him* about the diary. Even if we can't find out about Sarah, it's still a good story! He could come up to Toowoomba and film it at *Penzance.*"

"It'd be good publicity for your mum."

"Well, yes, it would be. *Fantastic* publicity! What d'you think?"

"I'll write to him, if you like."

Knowing, as I spoke, that it would never happen. Even though it was a great idea and just the sort of thing my father liked to grab with both hands. Like that Banjo Patterson thing. But I'd already written to him about it, weeks ago. And I'd had no reply. Not a word.

The truth was that Dad was living with some chick years younger than he was. So perhaps he didn't want reminding that he had a fifteen year old daughter. Or perhaps he didn't want her to find out.

We found everyone sitting in the parlour. Allie was pouring tea. She looked up. "Have fun, darlings? Did you find what you were looking for?"

"Not really, no," said Greg. "You don't want tea, do you, Kirsty? I'll get us some soft drink."

They were discussing opening day.

"It'll be at least the middle of February," Allie said, pulling a face. "There's still a lot to do."

Greg walked in carrying two cold cans. "We should be able to manage it before then, Ma."

"Yes, but remember I want to invite everyone for dinner. Everyone that's helped, I mean. And that has to happen *before* we open. You are all invited, of *course!*"

"Sounds wonderful," said David. "When's it going to be?"

"The kids go back to school at the end of January," said Mum. "Can you make it before that?"

"The last weekend of the holidays!" said Allie. "What d'you think, Greg?"

Greg thought for a moment. "Gives us a fortnight," he said. "We should be able to manage."

Mum leaned forward. "She hasn't told you the best bit. We've decided to dress up! On opening day. What do you think of that?"

Greg glanced across at me and I read the answer in his eyes. For once his opinion exactly matched my own.

When I got home I set to work transcribing the last part of Sarah's diary so I could give it to Greg the next time I saw him. I was intrigued by his idea that Sarah might be Lottie's mother. It made Sarah, that oddly lonely figure on the edge of the Greenaway family, seem much more real. And I wanted to know that everything had worked out all right for her. That she was okay.

"1st January 1893.

Last night there was a big dance in the barn to see in the New Year. Everyone was invited, including the people from the houses round about and all the servants. I recognised people from several neighbouring families who had visited us during the summer and others that I had met in town. There was a mob of boys who arrived on horseback and appeared to be friends of Drew's."

Sarah saw Eric Potter walk in by himself - his wife was still in bed after having her baby - and station himself by the supper table in the best position to look down the dresses of the young ladies. Or, at least, she assumed that's what he was doing. He was there most of the night and she never saw him eat a thing.

Dressed in her green and white striped dress, Sarah danced with Angus and Drew and several of Drew's friends. She danced with Papa and Uncle John. She managed to avoid dancing with Walter. Mama was on the floor all evening, her face red, her hair coming loose and looking years younger.

Meggie, looking happy and flustered at the same time, danced with her beau, Rory O'Neil , and at the end of the dance she brought him over to where Sarah sat with Martha and Grandmamma. He had brown eyes and full lips over strong teeth and a soft Irish accent. He held Meggie's hand very tightly in his own which was strong and hard and stained with dirt.

Sarah asked Grandmamma what he did and she said she thought he was one of the gardeners and she would have to see what she could do about finding them a cottage.

Walter spent most of the night with a group of people sitting on the other side of the barn. Grandmamma told Sarah they were the Beauchamps who owned a property called *Westerways* which skirted *Penzance's* southern border.

Martha nodded towards a small, dark-haired girl showing off a dainty figure in a white muslin dress. "That's Estelle. You remember? I told you about her and Walter."

Sarah watched Walter and Estelle stand up to dance. Estelle reached no higher than Walter's shoulder and danced as light as a feather. Sarah saw her look up and laugh at something Walter said and hated her on sight.

"She'll inherit *Westerways* one day," Martha said into Sarah's ear. "She had an older brother but he died a few years ago."

Grandmamma snorted. "The Beauchamps boy? He was never the slightest bit of good to anybody, that lad. Ran off to north Queensland - to the goldfields - after fighting with his father. Died of dysentery. He was in debt, too. Fancy running away to the goldfields and ending up in debt!"

"It just means Estelle has beauty *and* property," said Martha. "So it's no wonder the boys flock around her." She tossed her head. "Walter will marry her, if he can. He can't have *Penzance*. That'll be Drew's. But the place next door wouldn't be so bad. Though I wouldn't fancy Mrs Beauchamps as a mother-in-law."

Martha nodded across the room where the lady sat laughing loudly and fanning herself rapidly with some sort of feather contraption that she had taken out of her bag.

"She'll be your sister." Sarah stared across the room to where Walter and Estelle sat a little apart from the rest of the party with their heads close together.

Martha pulled a face.

At midnight the usual wishes and kisses were exchanged. Eric Potter left his place by the food table and went around the room getting his fair share.

To avoid him, Sarah got up from her seat and went outside. The air was cool and a new moon lay tangled amongst the branches of the trees by the gate. She looked up at the sky where the stars hung like yellow lamps. She felt tired and alone. She turned to go back inside and was surprised to find Walter leaning in the doorway, watching her. He pushed himself upright and came towards her.

"What are you doing out here, Sarah? Making a wish?" He indicated the new moon.

"If I was, *you* wouldn't be a part of it."

He stared down at her. "Maybe we ought to make a New Year's resolution to be kind to each other. What do you say?"

A small shrug. "Suits me. I didn't start it."

A piece of Walter's dark hair had fallen into his eyes and he reached up to scoop it back into place.

"Grandmamma told me what happened at the washpool. It seems I was wrong. About you at any rate. There's seldom an excuse for the way my cousin behaves." He put his hand gently under Sarah's elbow. "Come back inside, Sarah. You're missing the toasts."

Sarah allowed herself to be led back into the barn. She tried to ignore the sensation of Walter Greenaway's warm hand on her bare skin.

6

On Tuesday evening I rang Greg.

"How do you feel about Sarah and Walter?"

"You're *kidding*? Why, what's happened?"

"They had a bit of a chat outside the barn on New Year's Eve."

"A bit of a *chat*? Is that all?"

"I know it's not much," I conceded. "But they've decided to stop fighting. A New Year's resolution for 1893!"

"Maybe we should do the same. I don't mind if we kiss and make up."

I giggled. "Give up, Greg! Hey, listen, I talked to David about Lottie. He said to ask your Mum if she's got Lottie's birth certificate. That'd have the names of her parents on it. Or even her marriage certificate. Then at least we'd find out what her name was before she got married."

"Mum doesn't have any of Lottie's papers. I already asked her. Mr Brownlow, the solicitor, has got them all. She won't get them until she's paid his bill."

"She's going in to see him at the end of the week, though, isn't she? To sign the papers for the house? David said to ask her to take a good look at the title deed before it gets sent away. Or, better still, tell her to get a photocopy."

"What will a copy of the deed do for us?" Greg's voice was warm in my ear.

"David said we could find out who Lottie got *Penzance* from. If it was left to her in a will, for example, and, if so, who by."

There was silence at the other end of the phone.

"Come on, Greg! It'd be a start. I know you're in a tearing hurry."

"Why d'you say that?"

"Because you always are. What time are you picking me up tomorrow?"

"Mum's got an appointment at eleven. In the city."

"About ten, then?"

"You'll be lucky. Knowing Mum."

"See you tomorrow."

I hung up the phone and went into the kitchen. Mum and David were at the movies and the house was empty. Bats squeaked in the trees. A car accelerated up the street. I took a can of soft drink out of the fridge and stared out of the kitchen window at the dark night. I was thinking about Greg Hall. What was it about him that attracted me one minute and had me running in the opposite direction the next? Is that what it was like for Sarah and Walter? There was something about the way they behaved towards each other that made me wonder. But the diary was finished now, the rest of the pages lost to soot and damp and old age. Lottie's papers were the only clues we had left.

Allie arrived at quarter to eleven, tooting frantically.

"Is this where you live?" asked Greg at the door.

"Well, obviously."

"Come on, then. We're late!"

Allie dropped us off at South Bank. "Are you sure you'll be all right getting home by yourselves? Wouldn't you rather get a lift home with me?" She leaned out of the car window.

"We'll be fine, Mum." Greg swung his backpack onto his shoulders. "We don't know where we're going to end up, do we Kirsty? So it'll be easier if I catch the train. Don't *worry*."

"There's a train to Helidon just after three. Then you can catch the bus up the Range. Just don't miss it, Greg, because it's the last one."

Greg leaned down and gave his mother a quick kiss. "Go and get your work done, Ma. You're late already."

"Have a good time, darlings!" Allie wound up the window and nosed the little car into the traffic.

"Let's go and have a look at this South Bank place, then, shall we?" Greg turned away from waving at his mother's car. "Have you ever been here before?"

I shook my head.

"Neither have I. Mum said there's a beach here somewhere," said Greg.

"A *beach?* You're kidding! We're in the middle of the city."

"No, look! Here it is."

We rounded a corner and there in front of us lay a patch of impossibly blue water, surrounded by trees and gardens and full of little kids. A narrow beach of white sand held sun-bathers, lovers, and mothers with strollers and huge bags. Beyond was the wide brown river and a jagged skyline of city buildings. The smell of sausages and onions lingered in the hot air.

Greg took off his backpack and dumped it on the sand. "You gonna swim?"

"I haven't brought my togs. Anyway, who'd want to? In *there?*"

"Oh, yeah, I was forgetting. You're a real swimmer, aren't you?" Greg pulled his tee-shirt over his head, revealing a lean, tanned body.

"Was."

Greg glanced at me. "It's not the end of the world, you know, Kirsty. You can always go back, if you want to."

"That's easy for you to say. You don't know what it's like."

Greg wrapped his arms around his updrawn knees. "I was going to be captain of cricket this year."

"You can still play cricket. What's stopping you?"

"I can still *play.* I'll be lucky to make the Firsts, never mind captain."

"But why? If you're good?"

He turned his head and stared me.

"Come on, Kirsty . At a new school?"

"Do you mind?"

"Yeah, I mind. Of course I do!"

"It's not fair, is it?"

He shrugged. "Nothing's fair."

I reached down and dug my hands into the hot sand. "Do you miss your dad?"

"I don't really remember what he was like before he got sick. I just remember what Mum went through nursing him.

In a way I'm glad she doesn't have to do that any more. What about you?"

"I try not to think about him."

"But, Kirsty, at least he's *alive*."

"So what does that do for me?"

"If you want to see him you can. That's all I'm saying. "

"Sometimes I think you're better off if they're dead." I stared across the sunlit lagoon until black spots started dancing in my eyes. "If they're dead you can do the mourning bit, out in the open where people can see, then put them away in your heart or wherever, somewhere safe where you can remember them. Remember that they loved you." I turned my head. "That's what you've got that I haven't, Greg. Your father loved you. Still does, probably, from wherever he is."

He reached out his hand but I flinched away.

"Do you know what it was like when they split up? They argued about the CDs, about the pictures on the walls, about who was going to have the lounge and who was going to have the bed. They didn't argue about me. When Mum decided to come to Queensland I just kinda got packed up with all the other stuff. Sometimes I wonder - what if I hadn't packed my stuff into all those cardboard boxes that were lying around the place? What if I hadn't got into the car the day she drove away? Would I have been left behind in that empty house with the old magazines and the fluff in the corners?" I rubbed the back of my hand roughly across my face. "I'm sorry, Greg ..."

"What happened to your dad?"

"Oh, he had some girlfriend. The last in a long line, Mum reckons. So he just moved in with her."

"But you keep in touch?"

I laughed. "He does a good line in birthday cards and fifty dollar notes. Mum's not much better. Twenty dollars for pizza and a promise to go shopping at the weekend is about the best she can manage."

"On your *birthday*?"

I nodded. "But it's not *her* fault. She's trying to build her career. She told me that. Told me I'd have to be ..."

"... mature. And understanding."

I turned my head. "You get that, too?"

"My word I do." He imitated his mother's voice. "Darling, I've decided to have a go at *Penzance*. What do you think? Let's move from Sydney and live in some town in Queensland that you can't even *spell*. Lets forget about playing in the Firsts and ... and being a Senior at the school your *father* went to. And you're supposed to be *mature* and *understanding* about it! I'm only sixteen, Kirsty! What does she *expect*?"

I reached over and put my arm across Greg's hunched shoulders. He turned his head. His face was very close to mine. A moment of panic, an instant of doubt. Then our lips touched. The blue sky, the palm trees, the city sky-line across the river were replaced by the throbbing red of my closed eye-lids. And, behind my eyes, my mind churned with conflict.

It was the smell of onions that roused us. Greg's stomach, forgotten for a short while, was vying for attention. He reached for his shirt and pulled it over his head.

"D'you wanna eat? Mum's packed a picnic."

"I thought we'd grab a burger. Mum gave me twenty bucks."

Greg grinned. "Even better!" He stood up, pulled a plastic wrapped parcel out of his backpack and dumped it in the nearest bin. "You can have too much of a good thing, you know."

Hand in hand we crossed the river by the Victoria bridge, stopping in the middle to lean on the railings and stare down at the brown water. On one side South Bank crowded the river bank. On the other, the towers of the city woven into place by the tangled roads of the expressway.

"It's not a patch on Sydney harbour." Greg turned round and leaned his back against the railings.

"Let's face it, not much is. It's not bad, though."

"Glad you came?"

"Yeah. I've never been in the city before."

"I'm glad, too." He leaned forward and kissed me briefly. "Come on, Kirsty. I'm starving!"

The mall was crowded. Mums with strollers jostled with gangs of kids and little knots of anxious tourists. Bush ballads from a busker with a cockatoo on his hat competed with the whine of a violin played by a soberly-dressed Conservatorium student. The heat was like a relentless hand pressing us into the pavement.

The nearest hamburger place was underground and noisy and seemed to act as a passage from one street to another. We sat opposite each other on padded vinyl seats and ate hamburgers and chips. Underneath the table our knees touched. Greg was looking ridiculously pleased with himself.

"Are you looking forward to next weekend, Kirsty? Mum's big dinner!"

"It's not the one we have to dress up for, is it?"

Greg shook his head. "Not this time. A nice little pair of shorts would be just fine. Then I can ogle your legs."

"Yeah, that'd be right!"

"I must remember to tell Mum about the title deed. If she can grab it Friday, we can all take a look when you come up."

"You're still keen on this Sarah thing?"

"Of course I am!" Greg ate his last chip and wiped his fingers on a paper napkin. "You know something, Kirsty? I've never actually seen this famous diary of yours."

"It's not much to look at. It's been stuck up a chimney for a hundred years."

"Yes, but I'd still like to see it. After all, it's what brought us together." Again, that ridiculous grin.

"I'll bring it up at the week end, if you like." I glanced at my watch. "Hey, we'd better be going. What time train are you supposed to catch?"

"I think it was at three o'clock."

We squeezed out of the booth and made our way up the steep stairs that led to the street. We asked an old man the way to the railway station and received a complicated reply. At the bottom of the mall we turned left into Edward street. The next intersection was full of people dodging across the road in every direction.

"Which way?" I was panting from the walk.

"This way. Come on!"

"But we haven't got time!" Already the walk sign was blinking.

"Yes we have!" Greg grabbed my hand and dragged me diagonally across the intersection. As we reached the far pavement the traffic reclaimed the bitumen, council buses coughing fumes into the hot air.

We stopped outside the small shop of a coin dealer, staring through the window while I regained my breath. The window was full of packs of coins and old medals in faded cases. Flat pieces of wood with old pennies stuck in the end were advertised as two-up souvenirs. A faded type-written card explained the game.

I leaned my head against the dusty glass.

"Martha had a penny once. She kept it in the top of her stocking. She never could decide what to spend it on."

"What do you mean, in the top of her stocking?"

"They used to wear woollen stockings, heavy things, rolled up just above the knee. They'd twist the top around and make a sort of knot on one side then tuck the knot in, to keep them up. Martha used to keep her penny in the knot."

"It must have been uncomfortable."

"The whole lot must have been uncomfortable! Imagine thick stockings and ankle boots in this weather? To say nothing of two petticoats and a dress with three yards of material in the skirt! Shorts are a much better option." I glanced sideways at Greg and he grinned back. "Anyway she lost it in the end. The penny. She thought Bertie had stolen it. There was an awful row."

'So what did happen to it?"

I shrugged. "I dunno. Martha was never very careful with her things."

"Maybe it rolled under the bed. Have a look, when you get home."

I shivered. "What made you say that?"

"I dunno. Just a joke. Why?"

"It gave me the creeps, that's all."

"Hang on, you've got dirt on your nose." Greg leaned forward and rubbed my nose gently with one finger. "Okay? Ready to go?"

Further up the street we came to Anzac Square, crammed between buildings. "This way," said Greg. "A park and then a tunnel. That's what that old man said."

At the far end of the park a double flight of steep steps led up to a circular area where the eternal flame burned. Greg turned to me. "You wanna go up?"

I shook my head. "You go, if you like."

I sat on the edge of a raised pool and dipped my hand in the scummy water until Greg returned, taking the steps two at a time.

"It's cool! You should have come. I wonder what makes the flame work?"

"Typical," I said, getting to my feet. "Come on, we've got a train to catch."

We went into the tunnel past a skinny young man in a torn denim shirt who was singing Ben Harper songs, a scatter of coins in the upside down baseball cap at his feet. A few steps into the gloom and there was an open door in the tunnel wall, letting out a whisper of cold air. Inside, a hollow cavern of light reflecting from floor and walls. We peered in.

"What is it?"

"It's the war memorial." An old man in some sort of uniform stood just inside the door. "You can come in, if you like."

Greg peered at his watch. "We've got ten minutes.

It was cold inside. Freezing. The light claimed us, shining from ceiling and floor and walls. It was quiet. Only ourselves and the old man by the door. Names ran like a frieze around the walls. Borneo and El Alamein. Antwerp and Dieppe. Ypres, Somme, Gallipoli.

"I wonder if any of them are here." Greg stared at the soldiers' names marching in ranks down gold-trimmed boards,

"Who are you talking about? I don't know anyone who fought in a war."

"The Greenaways. I wonder if any of the Greenaways are here."

He was scanning the names eagerly. "They must have fought. Drew and the two little kids. What were their names?"

"Bertie. And ... and Jack."

"Bertie. Bertie. No, it would have been Albert, wouldn't it?"

I followed him from board to board. Names of regiments. Dates of battles.

And then, "Look here! Albert Henry Greenaway. And here, further down. Jack William. They must have joined up together. Died at Gallipoli, the pair of them."

"What about Drew?"

Greg shook his head. "Not here. There are more around the corner."

We found the name. Andrew John. In a regiment that fought in France.

"Oh, but that's awful!" I clutched Greg's arm. "Three of them. All dead."

"Who else was there? What about Walter?"

I shivered. "Let's go, Greg. It's cold in here."

"Hang on, Kirsty. Just let me look."

We searched the boards. Walter wasn't there.

Outside the hot afternoon air enveloped us. Greg grabbed my hand and we began walking up the dusty tunnel towards the station. "Well, so much for my theory about Sarah being Lottie's mum. I mean, if they all *died,* who did she marry?"

We arrived at the platform in time to see the back of a departing train disappearing into the sunlight at the end of the tunnel.

"Looks like you've missed your train," I said unnecessarily. "What are you going to do now?"

Greg grinned down at me. "Stay at your place?"

I grinned back. "You can if you want to. There's only the lounge to sleep on. We haven't got any spare beds."

"That'll do fine. I wonder what your mum's cooking for dinner? I'm *starving!*"

When Mum got home from work Greg and I were sitting in the front room eating slabs of bread covered with peanut paste and laughing at the quiz shows on TV.

After greeting Greg she said to me, "Come into the kitchen and talk about dinner."

In the kitchen she reached into the fridge and showed me a plate containing three large pork chops wrapped in cling film.

"Look!"

"Yeah, chops. What's the problem?"

"Yes, but there are only three of them, Kirsty. Greg's a sixteen year old boy. How am I going to fill him up?"

I giggled. "You make him sound like some sort of alien."

David walked in with a bottle of wine in his hand. "How hungry can he be? He's already eaten half a loaf." He bent over and gave Mum a kiss. "Look, why not just chop them up and make a stir fry?"

"That's one solution. Go and ask him, Kirsty, will you?"

Greg came into the kitchen with his empty plate which he dumped into the sink.

"What do you want, noodles or rice?" I asked him. "Mum's making a stir-fry."

"*Excellent*. Noodles, please."

"Well, that solves that problem," said David. He pulled the cork out of the wine bottle and handed Mum a glass. "So what about you two? Did you have a good day?"

"It was an interesting day." Greg answered for both of us. "Of course, the Greenaways were there, too. It's a bit hard to get rid of them when you're around Kirsty."

"We went into the war memorial near the station," I said.

"The war memorial? What were you doing there?" Mum sat down and began chopping vegetables.

Greg grinned. "Missing my train, for a start!

"We just went in for a look," I said. "We didn't expect ... Greg said to look for the Greenaways. He figured the boys would have fought in the First World War."

"Did you find any?" David sat down at the table.

"There were three of them. Drew and the two little boys, Bertie and Jack."

"Oh, but that's *terrible*," said Mum. "Their poor families."

"What about the other one," asked David. "The one who was going to be a doctor?"

"Walter? We didn't find him."

David sipped his wine. "All the same it raises a few questions. Like, if both of Uncle John's sons were killed, who did he leave *Penzance* to?" He turned to Mum. "The kids want to find out who Lottie was. See if there's a connection between her and the people in Kirsty's diary." Back to me. "Kirsty? What do you think?"

'If Jack and Drew were both killed that only leaves Anne. But I don't think she would have lived long enough to inherit anything."

"What was wrong with her?" asked Greg.

"She had tuberculosis. Consumption, they called it. Mum said it was common in those days."

"Well, tuberculosis certainly killed a lot of people," said David. "Carried on doing it until the '40s when penicillin was discovered. I had a great-aunt who died of it."

"So the possibility is that Uncle John lost all his children one way or another." Mum screwed up her eyes as she sliced into an onion.

"What would he have done?" asked Greg. "If there was nobody left to inherit the property?"

"Maybe he sold it. Most of the land was sold at some stage in any case. There are houses all round *Penzance* now."

"*Sold* it? I hadn't thought of that. But that would mean that Lottie wasn't related to any of them."

"No, but hang on," I said. "Drew was sixteen when Sarah's diary was written. That was 1892, right? And when did the First World War break out? 1914, wasn't it? Don't you see? That's twenty years. Drew would have been in his late 30s when he was killed in France. He could have had a tribe of kids by then. The rate he was going he probably did."

There was silence around the table.

"I always thought it'd be him," said Greg finally.

"Well, we'll just have to wait and see, won't we?" Mum scraped the last of the vegetables into a bowl. "Now how about a shower before dinner, you two? You've just about got time, if you hurry."

"I'll go first," I said to Greg. "Then I can give Mum a hand with the dinner."

I stood under the shower feeling the sharp sting of sunburn on my shoulders. It must have happened when Greg and I were sitting at that funny little beach at South Bank. When we kissed for the first time. I wriggled my shoulders under the hot water. It had felt so good - so right - when we were in the city. And it was what I wanted. If I was honest, I'd wanted it since the day we first met. But, now I was home, all I felt was a strange sense of unease. And that old familiar desire to be rid of him.

When I'd finished in the bathroom I went into my bedroom to put on clean shorts and a tee-shirt. I came out of my room, heading for the stairs. There was Greg half-way up, standing on the half-landing where the round window was, the one with the stained-glass pattern that David and I had put in for Mum's Christmas present. The late afternoon sun was streaming through the glass and Greg was standing in the middle of the coloured light

But it isn't Greg. This is a tall boy in dark clothes. He has deep brown eyes and long dark hair, springing from a peak above his forehead and touching his high, white, old-fashioned collar. I know who he is. He is the other boy, the one who lives in the shadows behind Greg's face. The one who makes me feel uncomfortable every time we are together. He looks up at me and smiles and I have an urge, almost irresistible, to run down the stairs into his arms.

But I can't move. My head roars with the sensations which have been my daily companions for months past, pushed down beyond thinking. The thump of a piano. The echo of laughter. The smell of tobacco smoke drifting through an open window. I look down the stairs and remember suddenly how I used to see coloured light falling from the window before David and I put the stained glass in and how it made me feel good to stand with the light all around me.

Greg moves out of the light. The other boy is gone.

"Have you finished in the bathroom? I've just got time for my shower." And then, when I neither move nor speak, "What's up? Kirsty, what's *wrong*?"

He takes a step towards me and I flinch from his touch. I don't want him near me. He knows it, too and he is not pleased. I don't know much about boys but one thing I do know is that they hate girls who blow hot and cold. But it isn't my fault. Not my fault that I spent all day with a boy, kissed him and let him hold my hand, and now I don't want to have anything to do with him. Because I saw a ghost on the stairs. Or thought I did

It was an awkward meal. Mum and David drank their wine and talked. Greg and I said nothing. Across the table his dark eyes stared at me, full of hurt. In the end Mum turned to me.

"Are you okay, Kirsty?"

"I'm just tired, that's all."

Not just tired. I was afraid, too. Oppressed by the breathing silence of the old house, waiting beyond the brightly-lit kitchen and Greg, a living ghost, sitting at the table and pretending to be an ordinary boy.

And soon I was going to have to help him make up a bed in the front room where the music was and the smell of tobacco smoke. And see him again in the morning before I could take him out into the fresh air and get him onto a bus and away.

While all the time the other boy stared from behind his eyes and filled my heart with a wild joy and something else - something I didn't want to think about.

Not yet, anyway.

I went to bed but I couldn't sleep. At four o'clock I got up and went to the bathroom for a drink of water. All around me the house lay silent. White curtains stirred in a warm breeze. In the gloom of the stairs the window was a cool grey circle, letting in the first light of morning.

I went back to bed and cried into my pillow. But I didn't know why.

7

The invitation was typical of Allie. A piece of gold-edged card with fine writing in a black pen, requesting the pleasure of our company for dinner on Saturday, 30th January. On the back she had scrawled, "Come up Friday night, family supper when you arrive."

It lay in the middle of the table while Mum and I argued about it. Of course, I didn't want to go but Mum had other ideas.

"Of course you want to go, Kirsty! You must be looking forward to seeing Greg again."

With no response, she moved on to flattery. "But, Kirsty! You'll be the star guest! If you don't turn up Allie will be so disappointed."

In the end - inevitably - she laid the guilt on me. "Look, Kirsty, you're far too young to stay home by yourself for a whole weekend. If you don't go, neither will I. David'll have to go by himself. I don't know what he's going to say to Allie."

I capitulated. Faced with the prospect of a whole weekend of blame, I went upstairs to pack.

It was past nine when we got there and the house was a blaze of lights. Allie met us in the hall under a vast, glittering chandelier which cast sparkling light on the moulded plaster ceiling, cream walls and carved timber of picture rails and door frames.

An old Persian rug, glorious in colours of faded red and gold, covered the floor. By the door an antique hall stand with an oval mirror, the top already cluttered with letters and bunches of keys.

Greg seemed as reluctant to see me as I was to see him. We sat either side of the big steel table in the middle of Allie's new kitchen eating home-made lasagna and eyeing each other warily. It was just as well the grown-ups behaved like noisy children and didn't notice our silence.

After we had eaten Allie stacked the dishes in an industrial sized dishwater and set it chugging. Then, while the kettle was boiling for coffee, she went into her parlour and brought out the photocopy of the title deeds for *Penzance* which she had obtained from Mr Brownlow that afternoon.

David reached out an eager hand and smoothed the paper out on the table while Mum peered over his shoulder.

"Oh!" he said. "Well, this is interesting. Look, Kirsty!"

He handed the paper to me. It was an A3 sheet upon which had been photocopied an old document with torn edges, covered with writing. At the top was the Queensland crest. At the bottom, a series of blurred squares containing hand-writing. In the middle a lot of words which seemed to be some sort of description of the property, followed by a small hand-drawn map. Underneath the crest was a name. Anna di Allessi. And, in brackets, the word 'widow'.

There was total silence around the table.

Greg spoke first. "Who's Anna di Allessi?" He took the paper out of my hands and stared at it, as if willing it to become something else.

"Someone who owned this house in ... There's a date there somewhere, isn't there, Greg?"

"1942."

"But what does it all *mean*?" asked Allie. "I couldn't make head nor tail of it when I got it home."

But David wasn't ready to answer. He reached out and took the photocopy from Greg. "Wonderful, aren't they? What a pity they're things of the past. All this information is on computer now. Deeds and share certificates, all works of art in their own way, especially the older ones. And think of all the *history* that's been lost." He looked around the table. "Can you imagine people sitting round a table in a hundred years time looking at a computer print-out? Not the same thing. Not the same thing at all."

"David, do shut up," said Mum. "And tell us what it means."

"It's one of the drawbacks of the Queensland system," explained David. "In England, for example, you would get every piece of paper that had anything to do with a property right back to the very beginning. In this case that would be sometime in the 1830s when *Penzance* was first surveyed. In Queensland, once a new deed was issued, the old one was surrendered."

"So why were new deeds issued?"

"A number of reasons. One is because they got full." David pointed to the small squares full of writing at the bottom of the page. "There was a new stamp put on for every transaction. When the deed was full of stamps, front and back, they issued a new one. That was in the old days, of course, before computerisation. Now, it's just click, click and away you go."

"It's probably faster though," said Greg.

"Faster!" replied David, as if speed was the worst thing in the world.

"But that isn't what happened in this case?" said Mum.

"No, it looks like this deed was issued after the land had been subdivided. They'd have issued a deed for each new parcel of land, including what was left of the original. Ah, thank you, Allie."

He reached his hand for the cup of coffee she was holding out for him. Took an appreciative sip. He was enjoying himself.

Mum spoke. "What you're saying is that some time prior to 1942 this di Allessi woman acquired *Penzance* somehow - bought it or inherited it - only we can't tell what happened because the old deed was surrendered when this one was issued. And this deed was issued because she'd been selling off the land?"

"I think that's pretty much spot on."

"So where does Lottie Hall come in?" I asked.

"Well, let's see." David's fingers began to trace the small squares at the bottom of the page. "Ah, here we are. Mrs di Allessi died in 1948. Here's the stamp showing that probate was granted to the executor of her estate. And *here's* the stamp transferring the land to the beneficiary of her will. Charlotte Sarah Hall!" He sat back. " So now we know."

There was silence around the table.

"Yes, but where does that get us?" I asked. "Why did someone called Anna di Allessi leave *Penzance* to Lottie Hall?"

"Lottie could have been her daughter," said Mum. She turned to Allie. "Is that where Greg gets his dark colouring, d'you suppose?"

"I have absolutely no idea. Nobody ever said anything to *me* about Lottie being Italian."

"But this Allessi woman wasn't necessarily Italian," said Greg eagerly. "She might have *married* an Italian but she could have been an Australian. See? It says 'widow' here. So di Allessi must be her married name."

"Like *who* for example? We are talking Greenaways here, I presume!"

"Hang on, I'm thinking about it." Silence for a moment, then, "Okay, how about this? Sarah and Drew get married round about 1900. They'd have been in their twenties by then. They have a daughter called Anna, right? She inherits *Penzance* from her father ... *what?*"

David was laughing. "You just never give up, do you?"

"Well, it works, doesn't it?"

"Oh, yes, it works fine! Not a shred of evidence but don't let that stop you."

"And what about Sarah and Walter?" I said. "I told you I thought they were getting keen on each other."

Greg shook his head. "Doesn't work. Because Walter wasn't going to inherit *Penzance*."

"He might have. If everyone else was dead."

Mum said, "So this Anna Greenaway marries an Italian - though where she finds one on the Downs is anyone's guess - and dies aged ... what? Forty? So what did she die of at that young age?"

"Could have been consumption," I said. "David said it was still around in the 40s before penicillin kicked in. And it did run in the family. Look at Anne Greenaway."

Allie leaned forward. "Yes, and what about Anne Greenaway?" She reached out and patted Greg's hand. "I'm sorry, darling! I do like your story but I can't see why we need to invent a girl called Anna when we've got Anne Greenaway already."

"But the name's spelled wrong, Ma. The deed says Anna, not Anne."

"That's not significant," said David. "It was quite common for names to be copied down wrong in those days."

"If this is Anne Greenaway, she lived a lot longer than we thought," said Mum. "She would have been well into her sixties when this deed was issued."

"Let's not forget that this might be someone else entirely who bought the property."

"Yes, but an Italian on the Downs?"

"It doesn't seem very likely, does it?"

Then David's quiet words cut through the hubbub of voices.

"Really, the only thing we can say from this evidence is that Anna di Allessi and Lottie Hall were probably related in some way, seeing that Lottie was left *Penzance* in Mrs di Allessi's will. What Greg's trying to find out is who Lottie's parents were. Isn't that right, Greg?"

A nod.

"Then what we need is her birth certificate." He looked around the table. "Allie, Greg said that Mr Brownlow has all Lottie's papers. D'you think you could ask him if there's a birth certificate among them?"

"Oh, but that'll be *Monday,*" groaned Greg. "I don't think I can wait that long."

"No, he's coming to dinner tomorrow night," said Allie. "I can ask him then."

"Yes, but it'll still be Monday before we get it."

"Well, you'll just have to be patient, won't you?"

Mum stood up and went to the sink to rinse her coffee cup.

"I don't know about anyone else, but I'm off to bed. You too, Kirsty, I think. It's been a long day."

Two rooms in the new building were completed and I slept in one of them, facing the street, the smell of paint and new carpet in my nostrils. The bed was too soft and the plumbing made gurgling noises but apart from that I slept well, dreamed of nothing I could remember and woke to the unfamiliar sensation of morning sunlight falling in wide golden stripes through the blinds at the window.

It was a hectic day. Mid-morning Allie's crew arrived - her kitchen staff and the people who were going to wait on the tables.

They trooped cheerfully into the kitchen and closed the door.

Half an hour later the flowers were delivered, boxes and boxes of pink and white rosebuds, and Allie came out of the kitchen long enough to pull a box of small vases out of the huge carved sideboard in the dining room and dump them in front of Mum

"You don't expect me to do them, do you?" laughed Mum. I'm an *accountant*, Allie, remember? Hopeless with flowers!"

But Allie had no time to argue. "Just shove them in. They'll be fine!"

After lunch David fetched a large cardboard box from his car. Then he and Greg locked themselves in the dining room and proceeded to make a great many knocking and banging noises until Allie was almost frantic with impatience and curiosity. Just before five she could stand it no longer. She rapped on the door. "Let me *in*," she shouted. "I've got to start setting the tables."

The door opened a crack and David peered out. "Get the others."

When we were all assembled he opened the door and let us in. He was grinning widely. "What do you think?" All around the walls were photographs set in wooden frames. "I found them in the shed. Or, at least, the fellow who was doing the demolition found them and had the sense to put them to one side. Boxes and boxes of glass plates. These are only a few of them."

He put his hands on my shoulders and guided me to the largest photograph which he had hung over the sideboard. "Look, Kirsty! How much d'you bet this is the photograph Mr Greenaway took on Christmas day?"

Through the glass I can see a group of people under a tree. Women with large hats. Young boys sprawled on the grass. An old woman in the front with a fat baby on her lap. Behind me I hear Allie's laugh and the rattle of her bracelet, a snatch of rock music as the kitchen door is opened and closed but the sounds are far away. In my head is Papa's voice coming muffled from under the black cloth that covers the camera. "For goodness sake, boys, stay *still*. It's only for a little while." The sound of his voice is as clear as the scent of roses from Grandmamma's garden and the cloying taste of brandy sauce that is lodged at the back of my throat. I shake my head to dislodge the memories and move to another photograph, this time of a girl and a boy on horseback. The girl is wearing a dark, fitted jacket and a hat with a feather in it. She is riding astride. We stare at each other through the glass.

"Clancy's gone to Queensland droving and we don't know where he are."

Greg comes up behind me and makes me jump. "What d'you think, Kirsty? Good, aren't they?"

I put my finger on the glass and feel it cold and smooth against my skin. "Don't you think this girl looks a bit like me?"

But Greg has me by the arm and drags me across the room. "Come and have a look at the one I've found."

A young man in a dark suit. From beyond the glass his dark eyes stare into mine. The high, white collar of his shirt accentuates his narrow, handsome face. I know who he is. He is the boy I saw on the stairs at home with the coloured light all around him. I feel my heart beating high and quick in my throat and wonder if I'm going to be sick.

"Don't you think he looks like me?" Greg's voice grates into my mind. "Who d'you think it is? Drew?"

I turn to face him. "I don't know who it is, Greg. And I don't care. I'm sick of you going on and on about who you're related to and who you look like. Why don't you just leave me alone?"

I ran out of the room. The front door was open and I went out of the house into the humid, late-afternoon air where the light hurt my eyes. I sat down on the steps and put my head into my hands while the sounds in my head rocked and swayed.

A light touch on my shoulder. I turned around and looked up into David's friendly, rumpled face.

"I'm sorry, David. I spoiled your surprise."

"It's okay, Kirsty. I understand." David sat down next to me and put one arm awkwardly across my shoulder. "Everyone else has treated Sarah's diary like ... like a bit of after-dinner entertainment. No more than that. But it hasn't been like that for you, has it, Kirsty? And you're upset about Drew. And the little boys. It's understandable."

I tried to remember about Drew. He'd never been that important.

David handed me a folded handkerchief, smelling of laundry.

"You've got too involved. That's all there is to it. I know the feeling only too well."

I leaned briefly against David's shoulder. "Thanks, David."

"Okay, now?"

I nodded.

"Come on then. The guests will be here soon. Allie wants us to have drinks before they arrive."

Allie had cooked lamb as a reminder of *Penzance's* origins as a sheep station. But this was like no lamb that I had ever eaten before. Boned out, it was rolled around a savoury stuffing and baked in a flaky crust. Thick, juicy slices lay on our plates with a rich, sweet sauce made from some red berries drizzled over the top.

It was a hot, stuffy night. The dining room was filled to capacity and full of noisy good humour. Allie was everywhere around the room, supervising the serving of the meal, stopping here and there to talk and accept compliments, pulling corks from bottles and pouring wine with a practiced hand . She was like a brilliant butterfly, hair bright in the lamplight, a tasselled scarf tossed over her shoulders. Occasionally she would settle briefly at our table to sip wine and nibble at whatever was on the plate in front of her.

One time David reached out and captured her hand.

"Sit *down,* Allie! You'll wear yourself out!"

But she was up and gone and Greg said, "She'll be all right, David. She's enjoying herself. I haven't seen her looking like this since Dad died."

Another time Mum said, "Who's that funny old chap in the suit? Over there by the window."

Allie looked. "That's Mr Brownlow. My solicitor."

Mum laughed. "Well, he certainly enjoyed his meal. I thought he was going to eat the plate!"

"Perhaps I'll go and ask him about Lottie's papers while he's in a good mood."

I watched her cross the room to the table Mr Brownlow shared with a faded little woman and stoop to talk to him. Then she threaded her way back between the tables to where we waited.

"Well, what an amazing thing! Mr Brownlow's wife used to live just down the road when she was a little girl. She remembers an old lady who lived in *Penzance*. Why don't you two go over and talk to her?"

Greg eyed me warily across the dirty plates.

"It's okay," I said. "We can talk about it."

We pulled up a couple of chairs and sat at Mr Brownlow's table. He was a plump, soft-fleshed man of about sixty wearing a tartan bow tie in the collar of an old, well-washed shirt. His wife was small and thin, sitting very upright in her chair.

"Ah," she said when Greg introduced me, "so you're the girl with the diary. What fun you've been having!"

"Mum says you used to live around here when you were a kid," said Greg.

"That's quite right, I did. A brand new house down by the creek. My father was the bank manager in Drayton."

"According to the deed, most of the land was sold in 1942."

Mrs Brownlow nodded. "We moved in when I was about four. That would have been a couple of years later."

"And the old lady who lived in this house? Anna di Allessi? Mum says you remember her."

"I remember her very well indeed. My mother used to come over and drink coffee with her in the little parlour at the back of the house. Mrs di Allessi was the only person she knew who made real coffee. We were all tea drinkers in those days, of course." She stared around the brightly-lit room. "That's why I was so very interested when Reg told me we'd been invited for dinner. Because I remember the house so well, you see."

"What was she like?"

"Mrs di Allessi? A small, pale-skinned woman. Not well. She never looked very well. And she had these dark eyes that *stared* at you. I don't think she cared very much for children. She used to say to my mother, 'Don't let her touch anything', as if I wasn't there at all. She'd give me milk and little sweet biscuits and I'd just sit quietly and look around. That room was the most amazing place I'd ever been in! I'd have stayed there all day, if I could."

"What was so special about it?" I asked.

Mrs Brownlow smiled. "You have to remember that we lived very plain lives in the '40s and '50s when I was growing up. I suppose that's what made that room so special. You see, it was just crammed with stuff she'd brought back from Italy. Carved chairs with velvet seats. Gold-framed mirrors. Beautiful paintings. There was a cuckoo clock on the wall. I loved *that*! I learned to tell the time, watching that clock."

"You said she'd brought this stuff back from Italy? Was she Italian herself? What was she doing on the Downs?"

"No, no, she wasn't Italian. She was from round here originally. I remember she told my mother that *Penzance* had been in her family for years. But she was all that was left. It was quite sad really."

"So she didn't have any kids?"

Mrs Brownlow shook her head.

"No children. And her husband had died in Italy. She came back here at the end of '39 just before the war broke out. She'd had a couple of brothers but they died in the First World War. When you come to think about it, it's strange that she outlived them. She'd been a consumptive in her youth and her chest was never good. It was what finished her off in the end, her chest. A cold winter and down she went with pneumonia. Maybe that's why she lived in Italy for so long, to avoid Toowoomba winters. But she wasn't a bad age. She must have been well into her sixties when she died."

Greg leaned forward. "Do you know anything about her brothers?"

Mrs Brownlow tipped her head on one side. "She had their pictures on her wall. Handsome devils, the pair of them. She told my mother they'd marched from Toowoomba with the Dungarees and joined up in Brisbane. The younger one had a withered arm but he joined the Light Horse and went to Gallipoli all the same. Of course, they could all ride horses in those days and there were

94

plenty of young men on the land who'd lost limbs for one reason or another."

"He didn't lose his arm," I said suddenly. "That's the way he was born." I turned to Greg. "It *must* be her. It all fits. Even those staring eyes."

Allie arrived at the table with bowls of dessert. "What have you found out, you two?"

Spoon poised, Greg looked up at his mother. "It looks like you were right, Ma. Anna di Allessi was Anne Greenaway after all. But we still don't know who Lottie was. Except she wasn't Mrs di Allessi's daughter because she didn't have any kids. That's as far as we've got."

Mrs Brownlow reached out and patted Greg's hand. "Now don't you worry about a thing. Reg is going into the office first thing tomorrow morning to see what he can find among Lottie Hall's papers It's all *terribly* exciting, isn't it? I'm so glad I came!"

"But it's Sunday tomorrow," said Allie. "Please don't go to any trouble."

Mr Brownlow picked up his spoon. "Dear lady, after the meal you've just given me, *nothing* would be too much trouble!"

It was half past ten before the last guests departed, clutching the roses from their tables and pieces of celebratory cake, wrapped in paper napkins. It was another hour before the last of the kitchen staff banged out of the back door. Allie, eyes glittering like a cat's, sat at the kitchen table where David had put her, clutching a large whisky and watching anxiously as Mum made coffee.

Humming cheerfully, Greg moved around the kitchen straightening tea-towels and hanging big pink rubber washing-up gloves on plastic hooks. He pushed the button on Allie's radio, heard the sound of a newsreader, and turned it off again. He opened a large square plastic container and took a slice of cake from the ruin inside. "Cake, anyone?"

"No, and you shouldn't either," said Mum. "You'll have nightmares."

"Not me! Only happy dreams tonight."

"It *was* a success, wasn't it?" said Allie. "Mr Brownlow wanted to come back next week. He was devastated when I said we weren't opening for a fortnight!"

"Well, you could open the dining room, if you wanted to," said David.

But Allie shook her head. "No, no. There's too much to do. And I want a proper opening. We're going to dress up, remember?"

Mum swallowed her coffee. "I don't know about anyone else but I'm just about ready for bed. How about you, Kirsty?"

Allie looked up. "Thank you, Kirsty, thanks *all* of you for your help. I couldn't have done any of it without you." She stared down into her empty glass. "I think I'll have another one of those, David, do you mind?"

"'Night then."

I went out of the kitchen into the hall. The front door stood open letting in a breath of cooler air. I stood for a while on the step and watched a car go past, its headlights pale yellow under the luminous sky. Somewhere beyond the thick suffocating clouds rode the moon shedding its radiance.

Mum came out and stood next to me, leaning on the verandah rail. "You okay?"

"Yeah. Sorry about earlier on. I just lost my cool for a moment, that's all. You know how annoying boys can be."

"Are you sure you're all right, Kirsty? You've been very quiet the last few days." She reached out her hand. "I don't want you getting sick again. It's school next week."

"Don't worry. I'm fine."

She took a step towards me and hugged me quickly. "Go on, now, into bed with you. I just hope you'll be able to get to sleep. I didn't realise it was so hot. Thank goodness Allie decided to air-condition the kitchen."

"Well, we could always sleep in there."

"As a last resort, I suppose we could. 'Night, sweetheart. Sleep well."

"'Night, Mum."

In my room I turned on the bedside light and got undressed. The bed felt damp and unpleasant. Above my head the fan turned slowly, stirring the humid air. My eyes were hot and gritty with exhaustion but I knew I couldn't sleep.

The diary lay on the bedside table. I reached out and took it in my hands, feeling the rich soft leather of the cover. There was a small pencil with a gold top pushed into the spine. A red silk ribbon marked a place towards the end. I opened the book.

The words were easy to read. I wondered why I'd found them so difficult before. Black pencil hurriedly on cream parchment pages. Yellow candle flame dipped and swayed. Somewhere the zing! of a mosquito.

"2nd January, 1893.

I suppose we'd all imagined that Drew's absence from the Drayton races on Boxing Day had something to do with a girl. But we were mistaken. It wasn't a girl he had been chasing but a horse. He brought it home this morning. I was standing by the slip-rails at the time, talking to Angus who was indulging in a little weather forecasting."

"There's rain coming," said Angus, showing Sarah a busy line of ants climbing the post near where they stood. "See the eggs? They're moving their nest. Wouldn't do that unless they thought there was good reason." He tipped his head back and squinted at the thread of last night's new moon lying ghost-like against the intense blue of the sky. "And the moon, too, see? Lying upside down in the sky. Tipping all the water out. When it's the other way up, it holds it in and the weather's dry." He looked down at Sarah. "Don't suppose they have ants in Melbourne. But the moon will be there sure enough."

There was a sudden commotion on the other side of the paddock and Angus turned his head to see what it was.

"Oh, good Lord! Stay here, Sarah." And he vaulted over the rails.

On the far side of the paddock Sarah could see someone on a horse. The gate was half-open but it appeared that the horse was not going through it without a fight. Rearing and side-stepping and tossing its handsome black head it shied and backed off every time the rider managed to get it facing the right way.

Angus ran across the paddock and yanked the gate open as far as it would go. Then he approached the horse, put out his hand and in one easy motion grabbed hold of the horse's harness. He stood for a long moment while the horse quietened. Then he turned and led it through the gate and into the paddock. Sarah could see that the rider was Drew. Now the horse was quiet he had regained his composure and was sitting easy in the saddle. Angus spoke to him, quite angrily, and Drew spoke back. Sarah saw him shake his head fiercely. Then Angus shrugged his shoulders and walked back to where she was standing.

"That damned horse! I told him not to buy it."

"What's wrong with it? It looks like a beauty."

"Oh, yes, she's beautiful all right. But it's all show and no manners with that one. Anyone with half an eye could see that."

"What did you say to Drew?"

"Told him not to ride her. He said *I* had, which is quite true. I did ride her, at the Boxing Day races but I wouldn't care to ride her again. It's too dangerous with a nasty-tempered beast like that. I told him to get rid of her before his father found out."

"Well, he hasn't taken much notice."

Out in the middle of the paddock the horse danced a circle, tossed its head and then threw itself onto its back legs in a great arch of rage. Drew held on, his face glittering with excitement, then the horse gave a shudder, came back down onto four legs and, just before it bunched itself up to run, flicked Drew from its back.

With his foot caught in the stirrup, Drew was dragged along as the horse made its dash for the fence, his head bumping sickeningly on the stony ground.

This time it was Sarah's turn. She crawled awkwardly through the slip rails and raced across the paddock. She could hear Angus' feet pounding behind her. Other people were there, too, men who had been working close by and had heard the commotion.

Angus went to where the horse stood against the fence, snorting and rolling its eyes. By the time he reached the horse's head and held it firm, the men had arrived. They untangled Drew's foot and laid him gently on the dusty ground.

Sarah knelt next to Drew's head. She placed two fingers in the soft hollow of his neck. There was no pulse. His skin was pale. She looked up at the circle of faces. Located Angus. She motioned with her hand.

"Down here, Angus. I need your help. The rest of you back off and give us some room."

Quickly Sarah demonstrated what she wanted Angus to do. "Hands like this, right? One hand on top of the other, *here.* Lock your fingers. You're going to have to kneel up and put some pressure on. Now, just wait until I say."

Gently she tipped Drew's head back, locked her hand around his jaw and opened his mouth. She looked up at Angus.

"Now, five pushes and rest."

Then she laid her mouth on Drew's.

They were into their third cycle, Drew still with no pulse, when Sarah became aware of a shifting of the silent circle behind her back. Somebody was standing directly behind her, close enough for her to smell the stuff he wore in his hair over the dry tickling of dust in her nostrils.

"What the hell is going on here?"

It was Walter's voice.

I stop reading. I can feel my heart beating in my chest. I stumble out of bed and across the room. The window slides open with a noisy rumble. Outside the rain has started, a thin grey mist that obscures the lights of the houses across the road. I lean my arms on the heavy wooden railings and stare out into the wet night. My hand goes up to the gold chain I wear around my neck.

How could I have forgotten?

I am shivering now. I pull the door shut, close the blinds and crawl back into bed. With my eyes tight shut, I find myself back at the old *Penzance* in the thick heat of a summer afternoon, kneeling on the dusty ground with Drew's body lying in front of me and Walter's anger a palpable force at my back.

If you do as much lifesaving practice as I had done during

my days with the swimming club it becomes as automatic as breathing. I hadn't thought when I began my dash towards Drew that my actions would be misconstrued. Hadn't cared. But nobody in the nineteenth century had ever seen mouth-to-mouth performed. And nice girls didn't kiss boys, especially not in the middle of the day with the farmhands watching. But the important thing was to keep counting and check Drew's pulse every two minutes. Walter's anger could wait for later.

"Just stand back, will you?" I spoke between breaths, not looking up. And then, when he made a step towards me, I turned my head. "Back off, Walter. Can't you see I'm busy?"

There was a shifting of feet and a low grumble of voices. I heard someone telling Walter what had happened. But I didn't take much notice. Angus and I had been working for over five minutes and already my back was starting to ache. And there was beginning to be a nagging thought at the back of my mind that sometime I would have to stop. Because there was no ambulance on its way, no life-support system, no intensive care waiting at the hospital. The closest thing I had to medical help was standing right behind me and he was no help at all.

Under my fingers Drew's pulse flickered into life. I looked up at Angus. "No more now."

Two minutes later I felt Drew move under my hands. I sat back on my heels and watched his chest rise and fall of its own accord. Angus and I grinned at each other like a pair of silly children. Around me the men didn't move. I realised that they were waiting for me to tell them what to do.

"Go and find an old door or some planks or something," I said. "We need to move him but you'll have to be careful. He may have injured his spine."

Angus got to his feet and dragged me up next to him. There was a tearing sound as the skirt of my dress parted company from the bodice.

"Are you all right?"

"A bit wobbly." I looked down at my torn and dirty dress and laughed shakily. "I don't know what Mama's going to say. That's the second one I've spoiled in two weeks."

Angus put his arm across my shoulders . "I don't suppose she'll mind. Come on, let's go and find a cup of tea."

As we walked away, I glanced over my shoulder to where Walter stood with Drew lying at his feet. It was hard to decipher the look on his face. Rage? Frustration? Puzzlement? But I didn't care.

"You can take over now," I said. A little cruel, I suppose. I didn't care about that either.

8

Later in the afternoon Walter came to see me. I was in my room where Grandmamma had insisted I go, bed-rest being her cure for all ills. Not that there was anything wrong with me, of course, but I think she was happier with me out of the way just then. After all, she had enough to do with the household in uproar and me, once again, the cause of it. To say nothing of her favourite grandson lying unconscious in bed.

I was sitting in a chair by the window with a book on my lap when he strode in and stood in front of me.

"How's Drew?" I asked. "Have you been to see him."

"I've just been there now. You saved his life, you know that, don't you?"

"Yes."

"I couldn't have done it."

"No. But I was lucky."

I gave him that much. I thought he deserved it. What he was saying was not easy. For him, at any rate.

"But I'm a doctor. Going to be one anyway. And you're just ..."

"Just what, Walter?"

He took a step closer to me. "That's what I want to find out. Who are you, Sarah?"

I looked up. "I thought you knew that already."

"What do you mean?"

"I thought you knew who I was. You had your mind made up about it before you even met me."

He shook his head. "I only know what my father told me."

"Don't you believe him?"

He took a step forward. "It's not the truth. I know that."

"If I told you who I really was you wouldn't think it was the truth either."

"So it *was* a lie? What you told my father?"

"No, he knows the truth. He just hasn't told you what it is."

"So now you accuse my father of telling lies!"

"Look, Walter ... Sit *down*, will you? I'll get a stiff neck in a minute."

He crouched on the carved blanket box at the end of the bed and continued to stare at me.

"What your father told you is true enough as far as it goes," I went on. "I have come up from Melbourne. My mother and I've been in Queensland about six months. I have no father. Or at least not so as you'd notice. What else?"

"That you'd been ill. Came up here to the sunshine. There was no mention of your mother."

"That was just to explain my hair." I ran my hand over my head. *"Explain* it?"

"Why it's so short. And my mother isn't here. I *am* alone. Without your father's help I would have been in real trouble."

"You said your mother was in Queensland!"

"She is. It's just ..." I stood up. "We'd better go and talk to Papa. You're just like Martha, you know that? Never happy until you get the lot."

Papa was in the old shed behind the stables which he had made over into a dark room for developing his photographs. I pushed the door a little way and slid in through the narrow space, leaving it open for Walter to follow.

The shed was gloomy and smelt of old mice and strong chemicals. Papa was crouched over shallow trays set out on a rough wooden table against the far wall. He turned at the sound of our approach

"Ah, so you've been talking to Walter," he said to me. "I expect he wanted an explanation, like the rest of them. You know you set the cat amongst the pigeons out there this afternoon, my girl! Not that I'd wish it undone, of course. Not for a moment." He turned to his son. "Has she told you the story?'

Walter shook his head. "Not all of it."

"Well, she hasn't told me all of it either. But, still it's extraordinary, don't you think?"

Walter glanced at me. "She hasn't told me how she came to be living with the family. Is that the extraordinary bit?"

"Then she hasn't told you anything yet. Just wait a moment and we'll go and talk outside. These can wait until morning."

He turned to the table and began covering the trays of chemicals.

"And don't go lighting that pipe of yours in here, Walter, or you'll blow us sky-high. There, now, come on."

There was a bench outside the shed, facing a tree-choked valley. The sun was going down behind us, touching the air with a hint of coolness and laying long black shadows over the scrub. Walter stretched his legs out in front of him and filled the bowl of his pipe. He stuck the pipe in the corner of his mouth and felt in his pocket for matches. When the pipe was lit, he blew a stream of blue smoke from his mouth.

"All right then, what's the story?"

"If I told you Sarah was from another time, what would you say?"

Walter took the pipe out of his mouth, went to speak, thought about it for a moment and stuck the pipe back in. "Yesterday I'd have said she'd escaped from a lunatic asylum and you should be in one. But, after what I saw today, I'm not so sure. You believe her, of course? Do you have any proof, apart from her word?"

Papa turned to me. "This is what happens when you bring up your son to have a scientific mind. *Of course* I've got proof, Walter! Although you wouldn't be so sceptical if you'd seen her the day she arrived. In that *extraordinary* garment. What was it, my dear? Pink? With a picture of a cat on it, as I recall."

"It was my nighty, Papa. What I wore to bed."

"And I ruined it. Tore it up. Set fire to bits of it."

"Well, we're just about even. I spoiled another dress today. I don't know what Mama is going to say."

He smiled. "I don't think you need worry. You saved Drew's life. There'll be ten dresses tomorrow."

"So why did you set fire to Sarah's nightdress, Pa?" asked Walter. "I presume she wasn't in it at the time."

"No, no! Of course she wasn't in it! I took it to my friend at the woollen mills in East Ipswich. I wanted to find out what it was made of. He said it had come from no plant or beast within his knowledge. I've forgotten now what Sarah called it."

"Polyester."

"Yes, yes, that's the word," said Papa. "Poly-ester. Man-made. *Extraordinary*! "

"Not proof she'd come from another time though, Pa. Perhaps it's just another new invention. We *can* invent things for ourselves, you know. We're doing it all the time."

"But there are other things, son! Things that Martha saw."

"*Martha*? What's she got to do with all this?"

"Martha's been there, Walter! Not in the same sense that Sarah is here with us now. But she's seen the marvels of the twenty first century with her own eyes. Tele - television, is it, Sarah? A small box with moving pictures. *Coloured* moving pictures. They float through the air and get into the box. Sarah can't explain exactly how it happens. And what was the other one? Tele*phone*. Press some buttons and food arrives. In a hundred years we'll be able to do that, Walter!"

"That's *pizza*," I said. "It's not really that wonderful, Papa. You ring someone up and they deliver it."

"And what do you suppose powers these inventions, my lad? And, if you say steam, you'll be wrong. Electricity, Walter! *Electricity*."

Walter turned to me. "So what's the connection. Between you and Martha?"

"We share the same bedroom. Same room. Same house. Different time."

"And you decided, did you, to swap your time for ours?" The suspicion was still there deep in his eyes.

"No, no, Walter! It wasn't like that at all! Martha wanted to go to Sarah. Or ... or Kirsty, I suppose I should say, shouldn't I?"

"Kirsty? Is that your real name? So why call yourself Sarah?"

"They gave each other names, Walter. The sort of thing that young girls do. Kirsty became Sarah. And what was Martha called?"

"Melissa."

"*Melissa*. That's right. She was going to be Melissa and live in your house and then it would have been *you* that'd have all the explaining to do!"

"Yes, but it didn't work out that way."

"No, it didn't. You came here."

Walter said nothing for a while. He puffed on his pipe, watching the swallows darting around the building in the golden light. Eventually he turned to me. "See it from my point of view. I come home for Christmas to find a strange girl living with my family. My father tells me some cock-and-bull story about her being the daughter of an old friend from Melbourne. Which I know is untrue because I go to university with the chap's son and I know he hasn't got any sisters! You can't sew, can't paint, can't play the piano. But you do swim and you ride astride. Something I have never seen a young lady do. What was I *supposed* to think?"

"Look, son. *I* lied. Not Sarah. You should have come and talked to me about it instead of blaming her."

"But *why,* Pa? Why did you lie?"

"You can see why, can't you! Nobody would have believed the truth. I had to make a decision about what to tell the world. And I had to make it quickly."

"Yes, but why me too? Couldn't you have told me the truth?"

"It had to be everyone, Walter!" Papa reached out his hand and laid it on Walter's knee. "Look at the difficulties you're having with this! And there are a dozen farm hands out there who saw what you saw this afternoon. Are we going to tell them the truth? Or a lie they'll believe? And I had Sarah to think about, too. She had to be protected from gossip and speculation. And, if truth was the casualty, it was a small price to pay. I didn't know about the chap at university. So it wasn't even a clever lie, in the end."

Papa dug finger and thumb into his waistcoat pocket and brought out his watch. He held it in the palm of his hand and flipped open the lid. "Perhaps we'd better go and have some tea."

But neither of us moved. Finally, Walter turned to me and put out his hand. "It seems I owe you an apology, Sarah. Or should I call you Kirsty?"

A moment's hesitation then I reached out my hand to meet his. There was a long silence while we stared at one another. His eyes were dark brown and deep enough to drown in.

Then Walter smiled, the first time he had ever smiled at me and meant it.

And I smiled back.

I woke early the next morning, dressed quickly without disturbing Martha and went to the kitchen to beg some bread and meat. I intended spending the day away from the house and in peace. Before I left, I visited Drew's bedroom. He was awake, propped up on pillows and complaining about the pain in his head and the strength of the light coming in between the curtains at the window. His eyes were surrounded by navy-blue bruises, his skin the colour of skim milk. He remembered nothing about the events of the day before, or my part in it, which made him the only person this side of the Range who didn't know what I had done.

There was a small billabong hidden in the trees at the bottom of the back paddock. It was Jack and Bertie's favourite spot. They had a camp fire in a circle of stones and liked to cook lamb chops in an old black frying pan which they kept in a secret place, along with a battered billy. The billabong had waterlilies on it, blue ones, and there were brown ducks busy around the edges. A tall egret stood on the opposite side, contemplating its reflection. It was very quiet.

I had a stone bottle of ginger beer which I sank into the billabong to keep cool and a couple of paper-wrapped parcels of sandwiches and fruit cake wrapped up in an old tea cloth.

I was half-asleep on the grass when Walter found me

"What do you want?" I struggled to sit up.

"To talk."

"I don't want to talk. That's why I came down here. How did you find out where I was?"

He squatted down. "Mrs Armitage told me."

"She would! I only told *her* so Grandmamma wouldn't worry. Did she give you some lunch?"

"Of course!"

I nodded towards the billabong. "The ginger beer's over there, if you want some. I notice you didn't bring any of *that.*"

Walter tipped his head back and laughed. "She must love you more than me."

He got to his feet and ambled to the water's edge.

When we had finished eating, Walter said, "Do you know where the boys keep their billy? We can have some tea."

I left Walter to light a fire while I fetched the billy from the boys' hidey-hole and bent to fill it with water from the billabong. It was scummy and green near the edges and I took a step forward to find cleaner water. My foot sank into soft mud and I felt cold water fill my boot.

I squelched back to where Walter was feeding the flames of a new fire, dumped the billy on one of the rocks that formed the fireplace and bent forward to unlace my boot.

"What are you doing?" Walter was staring at me in horror.

"Taking off my boot. It's full of water."

"You can't!"

"Why not? I don't like having a wet foot."

"Because *I'm* here."

"Oh, don't be so silly, Walter! It's only a foot. Turn around, if you don't want to see."

Walter turned his back on me. I unlaced my boots, pulled off my thick stockings and wrung muddy water from the toe of the wet one. I stood up and draped the wet stocking over a low branch.

"Can I turn around now?"

"If you like. I hope you're not offended by the sight of a girl's stocking because I've hung it in the tree."

It was blissful to sit with bare feet in front of that small fire with the blue smoke drifting into the warm air. Even Walter's presence didn't spoil my enjoyment. In fact, now that Walter seemed to have decided to add me to his list of okay people, I was beginning to understand what everybody else saw in him. I remembered the look on Mama's face when we came back from Aunt Dot's in the pouring rain and she saw him standing on the verandah with the kids and dogs clustered at his feet. How Mrs Armitage would let him take a hot scone off the plate before it was put on the table, something nobody else would dare to do. And Anne Greenaway at dinner making sheep's eyes at him through the candle flames.

"You're going to have to tell me, you know, Sarah." Walter was lying down again with his hands behind his head.

"Tell you what?"

"How you got here."

I turned around and pointed. "Down that little path, see?"

Another one of those wonderful laughs. "Come on, Sarah. You know what I mean."

I drew my knees up under my chin, wriggling my toes in the damp grass. How was I going to explain it to Walter when I didn't understand it myself? Sometimes I thought I was in the middle of some elaborate dream. Or some sort of ghost world that I'd fallen into accidentally. But these people were not like ghosts, or dream figures. They seemed so solid, so sure of themselves. And it was me who hovered, insubstantial and afraid, on the edge of their world.

I could hear an aeroplane high up in the blue sky, the sound a thin thread in the hot air. I didn't look up. It was something I had become used to. That and the murmur of traffic on the highway beyond the Greenaways' paddock . Sometimes I was afraid to go to sleep, scared of where I might find myself the next morning.

It hadn't been like that to start with. Then it had seemed no more than a game.

The first time I saw Martha was one evening at the tail end of winter just after Mum and I moved to Ipswich. I was in my room, watching the sun set behind the clock tower of the old school across the road. It was a glorious red and orange sunset with flags of dark clouds hurrying across the sky in front of a fresh westerly wind.

Just as the light went out of the sky the wind swung around and swooped through my window, setting the shadows jumping on the wall behind me. But surely that had not been a shadow?

The figure of a girl about my own age, but small and neatly-made, her hair long down her back. And, behind her head, was that wallpaper I could see on my cream-painted walls? A pretty paper with trellises of blue flowers.

She turned her head and seemed to see me. Our eyes met. She was as startled as I was.

But then Mum came in and snapped on the light. "What are you doing, sitting in the dark?" and the moment was gone.

I didn't see the girl again after that, not for a long while. The nights became cold and I spent less time in my room. We had discovered a fireplace in the living room downstairs – the first of the series – and we delighted in it, sitting in front of a blazing fire night after night with the wind roaring outside.

Spring came and quite suddenly the weather was hot. One afternoon the door to my room opened sharply and the girl walked in. Dressed in a loose, white frock, she tossed her straw hat onto the bed and walked rapidly towards the window. She had her hands under her masses of dark hair, lifting it away from her neck to cool it. She stopped, one step away from walking into, or through, me and stepped back.

"You again! What are you doing in here?" She had a low, firm voice with a hint of challenge in it.

"It's my room," I said. "Why shouldn't I be in here?"

"*Your* room? Don't be silly. And where did that desk come from? I've never seen *that* before."

Behind her head the blue flowers bloomed on my bedroom walls. The bed was draped with white covers. A mosquito net hung from the ceiling.

We stared at each other for a long moment.

But then she began to fade away and, blinking my eyes, I saw the cream paint and familiar furnishings of my own room.

After that I saw her often. I think she began to seek me out deliberately. She was obviously far more adventurous than I was for, although she fascinated me, she frightened me too and I was too afraid to ever try to summon her myself. She came in the quiet time of the afternoon when I was in my room, waiting for Mum to come home from work. She would come through the door with that determined step of hers, toss herself onto the bed, and engage me in breathless conversation.

We became so much a part of each other's thoughts during those weeks that she would often appear in bed as I lay in that half-state between sleeping and waking. Who summoned whom at those times I don't really know but we would lie cozily side by side and talk. And then in the night, if I woke up, she would still be there, turning and sighing in her sleep. They were the best times, the good times. But, as everyone knows, good times don't last forever

"So what did you think she was?" Walter was propped up on one elbow.

"I thought she was a ghost. Obviously. I mean, it *is* an old house, or it is for me. And she was wearing old-fashioned clothes."

I looked down at my own clothing. A print dress covering two lawn petticoats and one flannel, tied around my waist with tape. A battered straw hat to keep the sun off my complexion. Ankle boots and thick stockings, discarded in the grass.

"But ghosts are supposed to just hang around, aren't they, isn't that the whole idea? Whereas, with Martha, time was passing. In fact she seemed to be having an ordinary sort of life, just like me. School. Mealtimes. Arguing with Bertie. One day she had a bandage on her thumb where she'd cut herself peeling pumpkin. She can show you the scar, if you want to look."

"Papa said Martha wanted to come to you."

"She did. She was very keen on the idea."

One afternoon in late October, Martha came into my room. She made a grab for the remote which was lying on my bed but, as usual, she couldn't touch it. "Turn the TV on, Kirsty! I can't stay long."

I clicked the button and the screen brightened. Martha threw herself full length on the bed, cupping her chin in her hands. She was addicted to the afternoon soaps.

"It's Meggie's afternoon off and I'm supposed to be watching Ethel," she grumbled as the credits rolled.

"Why? Where's your mum?"

"Gone to Richies' for a card of shirt buttons that couldn't wait till morning."

"Well, she doesn't know you like to watch telly in the afternoons, does she?"

Martha giggled. "I suppose not. Now, shush, Kirsty. It's starting!"

When the show was finished she climbed off my bed and retrieved her hat which she'd tossed onto the floor. "I suppose I'd better be off. See you tomorrow, Kirsty."

She headed for the door. Then she turned around and walked back into the room twirling her bonnet round and round her finger. "It's not fair! I wish I could live here all the time!"

"You *do* live here, remember?" We'd had this conversation before and I knew where it was heading.

"No, I mean *really* here. With you!" The hat flew off her finger and landed in the corner of the room.

I bent down and picked it up. "Look, Martha, let's leave it, okay? Things are just fine the way they are."

"I can't see what's so wrong with it," said Martha grumpily. "Your mother won't notice. You said yourself she's hardly ever home." She lifted her heavy hair away from her neck. "I'm going to be Melissa and cut my hair and live here with you. I can eat pizza. Watch TV. And I won't have to play the piano ever again. I can hardly wait!"

"Hadn't you better be going? I thought you were supposed to be looking after Ethel." I held out her hat, aware suddenly of the feeling of rough straw between my fingers.

Martha grabbed her bonnet and stared up at me, her eyes full of frustrated energy. "Oh, don't be such a spoilsport, Kirsty! We could at least *try*." She stepped forward, reaching towards my hands. "Tonight at midnight. Think of me. As hard as you can. And I'll do the same."

"It won't work."

"It might. I'll see you tomorrow."

And she was gone.

I wasn't going to do it. There was no way. But at midnight I found myself awake. I lay, heart pounding, listening to the sounds of the night. The house creaked. A car accelerated up the hill. Far away thunder growled. After a while, I drifted back to sleep. I woke again towards morning. It was hot and stifling. The thunder was closer now. I could hear the hush of the rain and smell the wet earth through my open window.

The sun woke me next. It was hot and bright, diffused through the white netting that covered the bed. Martha lay asleep, the length of her body touching mine where we had rolled together during the night. I looked around. It was Martha's bed I was in. The sheets were a rough fabric which scratched my legs.

I crawled out from under the mosquito net and went over to the window. It was a fine, hot day with a few white clouds floating in a summer-blue sky. The house stood in fields. The road was now a rutted dusty track up which rode a boy on a big horse, whistling through his teeth and whacking with a stick at the tall weeds that grew either side of the track. The grammar school stood on the hill opposite, solid and familiar. All the houses around it had gone.

"What happened then?"

"Papa came in with his collar half off and saw me standing by the window in my pink nightie. And you know the rest."

"And Martha?"

I laughed. "She was *bitterly* disappointed. Because, with me here, she can't get her daily dose of the soaps."

"And ... soaps are?"

"It doesn't matter, Walter. They're not something you're going to have to worry about in your lifetime."

"And how did *you* feel about it?"

I shrugged. "It wasn't my choice to come. But I've been lucky, I know that. Papa - your father - has been very good to me."

A pause. Then Walter said, "My father is probably the only man in Ipswich who would listen to a story like yours."

"And believe it."

"Yes, that, too." Walter turned his dark gaze towards me. "How do you account for what happened, Sarah?"

I picked up my straw hat out of the grass, feeling its rough texture between my fingers. "I have no idea. I never really gave it much thought before it happened. Martha was around and that was fine but I didn't want to take it any further. And then - suddenly - here I was. I suppose I'd forgotten, or didn't think, that what was already happening between Martha and me was just as impossible as what Martha was asking me to do."

"You were already half way there."

"More than half way, I'd say. *What*?"

He was sitting up with his chin cupped in his hand, staring at me.

"Nothing. It's just that I'm beginning to understand how you've managed to bewitch every boy in the place. Do you know your eyes are exactly the same colour as the water over there?"

His own were very dark and very close.

I turned my head and stared at the quiet billabong and the afternoon sky with its fringe of storm clouds. I didn't want to look at Walter any more.

"Not every boy. It's only really Angus."

"Oh?"

"Drew fancies everyone. And I didn't mean to make Angus like me."

"Didn't mean to? Oh, that's rich! He's worth a fortune, you know, Sarah - Kirsty. You should snap him up while you can."

"Don't *you* start. That's what your grandmother said."

"Kirsty?"

"What?" I was aware of his hand in the grass almost touching my own.

Walter reached out and touched my face, very gently, with his outstretched finger.

"What would a twenty-first century girl do if she knew a boy wanted to kiss her?"

I turned my head. "It would depend ..." I cleared my throat. "It would depend on whether she wanted to kiss him."

"Do you?"

I didn't reply. I put my hand around the back of his neck and drew his face towards mine. It took Walter about thirty seconds to get over the shock. No, wait. Thirty seconds is half a minute. It wasn't as long as that.

I felt his arm come around my back to hold me and suddenly I was clinging, drowning, lost, my life reduced to a patch of damp grass, the hot sunlight on my eyelids and the strong arms of a boy, and it didn't matter any more which century I was in. It was as if everything that had ever happened to me in my whole life had been leading up to this one moment. Is that what you feel when you fall in love?

Ignored, the billy came to the boil, bubbling merrily and splashing into the flames of the fire. A kookaburra hopped out of the tree above our heads and pecked eagerly amongst the debris of our lunch.

Our lips parted. "Kirsty ..."

"What?"

"We shouldn't be doing this."

"Why not? It's only a kiss." Only a kiss? What was I saying? "But, if I go home with grass stains on the back of this dress, I'll be shot. No questions!"

"You were lying down before."

"Not with you on top of me, I wasn't."

"You want me to get up?"

"In a minute."

9

That was the last fine day for almost a week. For days afterwards the rain came down in a grey sheet and confined the family to the house. It didn't take long for me and Walter to discover that, even in a big house like *Penzance,* it is difficult for two people to be together and remain undetected.

Drew's health improved enough for him to spend part of each day lying on the sofa in the parlour with Martha playing nursemaid, feeding him with beef broth and bread sops and reading stories from English magazines when probably he would have preferred to be left in peace. At least it kept Martha from wondering where I was.

I spent the first wet morning helping Grandmamma sort the linen which was kept in a big wooden cupboard in a small room off the kitchen. The room had a stone floor and whitewashed sandstone walls but was warm because it shared a wall with the big kitchen range next door.

After an hour or so, Grandmamma went off to attend to some other business in the house. "What are you doing in here, Walter?" I heard her say as she went through the kitchen. "There's a fresh scone there, if you're hungry."

"I'm looking for Sarah, Grandmamma. There's a letter for her."

"She's in the linen room. But don't keep her talking. She's got plenty to do."

Moments later he appeared at the doorway with tea in a china cup and a fresh scone dripping with butter on a cracked saucer which he placed carefully on the table among the piles of linen. We gathered each other in - fingers, hands, arms, until we could get no closer. The kissing was hungry, hurried, almost painful in its intensity until we drew breath and moved a little apart.

"Have you really got a letter for me or was that just an excuse?"

"No, look, here it is. It's from Daisy. Come on, open it! What does it say?" He perched on the table, toppling a heap of tablecloths with embroidered corners.

I scanned the first few lines. "Lizzie's walking out with Arthur Duncan from the Building Society. He's been for tea but Uncle George said they can't get married for years because Arthur's only a junior clerk and he has to rise in the business before he can afford a wife."

"Arthur Duncan? I don't think I know him. What's he like?"

"I've never met him. Martha says he's got yellow whiskers and a cardboard collar. Whatever *that* means."

"It means he can't get his mama to starch real ones. Cardboard collars are *very* cheap, Kirsty! *I'd* never wear one. What else does she say? Eat your scone!"

I took a buttery mouthful. "Their Jimmy's coming up. Tomorrow. No, today! He should be here by now. Daisy says she hopes he'll be made welcome at *Penzance*, despite the little mishap last summer."

"What little mishap? What did he do?"

"Nicked Drew's nose with a stock whip."

Walter shook with laughter. "He didn't, did he? Oh! I'd like to have seen that!"

"Ask Drew to show you the scar. It's *very* fascinating."

"What's Jimmy doing on the Downs?"

"He's going to see the sergeant at Drayton. That's where he's going to be stationed when he's finished his training."

"Oh, yes, he's a policeman, now, isn't he? *Constable* James Sangster! That'll take a bit of getting used to. I hope he does come to *Penzance*. I haven't seem him for a long time."

"What's he like? I've never actually met him."

"Oh, you'll like him, Kirsty! Jimmy's a nice chap. But not as nice as me."

"There's nothing in the least bit nice about you, Walter Greenaway. I've told you that before."

He grinned. Slid off the table. Ducked his head and kissed me long and hard. "There! That was nice, wasn't it?" He laced his fingers tightly with mine. "*God*, this is awful. I wish there was somewhere we could go."

"Papa's in his shed. We can take his lunch down in an hour or so. Go and sweet-talk Mrs Armitage into doing him a tray."

"You're a genius." He kissed my forehead. "I don't think I can last an hour. Drink your tea before it gets cold."

Papa was very pleased to get a tray of cold mutton and pickle sandwiches instead of having to break off and come up to the house. He was in the middle of developing the Christmas photographs and the damp weather was playing havoc with his chemicals. He came out briefly to eat his sandwiches and slurp a couple of cups of tea from the big enamel pot then went back into the gloom leaving us to hold hands on the bench under the eaves with the rain from the roof pock-marking the dirt just beyond our feet.

The next time we met was at dinner time. Martha and I were to eat with the grown-ups that night because Aunty Dot and Eric Potter were coming over, the first time Aunty Dot had been out of her house since the birth of her son just before Christmas.

The baby, wearing a lacy bonnet and a long embroidered frock, was fat and red-faced just like his father. The only difference was that he objected strenuously to being handled by all the women who clucked over him as if he was the only baby that had ever been born. Eric Potter straddled his legs in front of the empty hearth and watched the proceedings with a self-satisfied smirk.

By the time the baby came our way he was damp and furious. Martha passed him hastily to me. I held him out in front of me and looked around for someone to take him away. Walter came across the room and scooped him up with one hand.

"What a dear little creature," he said, laughing and pulling a face.

Neither Drew nor Anne were well enough to eat with the family which meant a bit of fancy footwork when we went into the dining room. I was determined to take Anne's accustomed spot next to Walter. Martha was only interested in not sitting next to Eric Potter. There was almost a disaster when Walter made a dash for the other side of the table where I normally sat but Grandmamma's voice cut through the chaos.

"Walter, sit in your normal seat. You can have Sarah next to you instead of trying to talk to her across the table. You seem to have so much to say to each other these days. Martha, there! Eric, next to me."

"Do you think she knows?" I asked Walter, later. I had excused myself to go to my room for a handkerchief and had 'found' him on the verandah, where he said he was going to be, leaning comfortably against the corner post and smoking his pipe.

"Grandmamma? She wouldn't approve."

"Why not?"

"I'm supposed to marry Estelle Beauchamps. It's been arranged for ages. Between Grandmamma and Estelle's ma."

"Arranged? Don't you have any say?"

"Of course I do!"

"Do you want to marry her?"

"I thought I did. Last week I wanted to." He turned around and stared out at the rainy night. "She'll have *Westerways* one day, Kirsty."

"Yes, but do you *love* her?" The rain was blowing cold on my face.

"Love doesn't have anything to do with it. *Didn't* have anything to do with it"

"What do you mean?"

Walter put his arm across my shoulder and drew me closer. "Last week I didn't know what love was."

There was a sound at the other end of the verandah.

"Walter, is that you?" It was Uncle John's voice. "I need you to settle an argument." He took a step forward. "Who's that with you? Sarah?"

Walter turned his head. "She's got something in her eye. There, is that better?"

"Well, come into the light, lad. It's no use trying to do it out here in the dark."

"It was only an eye-lash. It's fine now." It was hard to keep the laughter out of my voice.

The Boxing Day concert had been delayed twice. First, because of the uproar caused by my swim in the washpool and again, following Drew's accident. Now, with a house full of people and the rain continuing to fall, Grandmamma decided to have a third attempt. We were into the last week of our stay at *Penzance* so there was no time to spend on renewed rehearsals. The date was set for two nights hence, ready or not. It gave Eric Potter a chance to leave Aunty Dot with us while he went off on pursuits of his own. She was desperate for a little fun and only too happy to abandon the baby to Meggie's care while she and Walter went into a huddle to rehearse an act they'd been performing together for years.

With Martha in possession of the piano and Walter and Aunty Dot locked away in the dining room, I went in search of Angus. I knew he wouldn't be anywhere inside the house so I crossed the muddy yard behind the kitchen and found him in the stables with the horses.

The black mare that had thrown Drew was in a stall at the far end of the stable awaiting Uncle John's decision regarding her future, and this is where Angus was.

I stood for a while in the yellow light of an oil lamp breathing in the smell of sweat and dung and straw. I watched Angus draw his big hand gently down the curve of the horse's neck and heard the murmur of his voice whispering sweet nothings into her quivering ear.

The horse was so intensely aware of Angus' presence that she was standing completely still, the only movement the shuddering of the muscles beneath her glossy coat. I took a step forward and the horse flinched, rolling her eyes.

Angus turned his head. "There's no hope for her, you know. It's a wicked shame."

"Why? What'll happen to her?"

He put two fingers to his temple and imitated the pulling of a trigger.

"Poor thing." I took a step forward. The horse shifted her head to keep me in view. "Can't you take her?"

"To Melbourne? I don't think so. Come on, Sarah. We'll go outside."

We sat on hay bales just inside the stable door, watching the rain.

"What about the concert, Angus? D'you still want to do some poems? We've only got a couple of days."

I could feel the straw pricking my legs and shifted uncomfortably.

Angus looked surprised. "I thought you'd be doing something with Walter."

I shook my head. "He's doing some sort of duet thing with Aunty Dot."

"I know all about you and Walter, you know, Sarah. He told me himself."

"What did he say?"

"Said he was in love with you. Forgot, I suppose, that I was in the same boat. But I wasn't that surprised. Not really. I've seen the way you look at each other."

"How?"

He turned his far-seeing, bushman's eyes towards me.

"You stare at him when he's not looking and he stares at you when you're not looking. It's been going on for weeks. Plus your sudden interest in photography."

"Photography?"

Angus grinned. "Hours on end down at the back shed with Mr. Greenaway. Don't worry, I don't think anyone else has noticed."

"Oh, Angus."

The trouble was I liked him. I liked him very much. But love is a funny thing and it was never going to be me and him, no matter how hard I tried.

"Not your fault if you like another chap better." Angus reached into the pocket of his old riding jacket and pulled out the battered book of poetry. "Which one do you want to do?"

"Any that aren't about horses. Or droving."

"But they're the only ones worth reading, Sarah. If they're not about the bush and horses and ... and that sort of thing there's not much point to 'em. I've been reciting them to Bess over there and she likes them well enough."

"We'd better do *Clancy*, then. We both like that one."

I reached out and took the battered book out of his hand.

"And it's kind of relevant, isn't it? To both of us. Me from Melbourne. You going there." I found the place. "Listen, Angus, this bit,

> *And in the place of lowing cattle, I can hear the fiendish rattle*
> *of the tramways and the buses making hurry down the street.*"

Angus groaned. "Don't, Sarah. I don't want to be reminded."

I laid my hand on his arm. "You'll get used to it."

He lowered his gaze to my face. "I don't think I will."

The following evening, after a boiled egg and a cup of tea amidst the bustle of the kitchen, Martha and I went to our bedroom to get ready for the concert.

"I was hoping we'd be able to dance tonight," Martha grumbled while Meggie tugged at her hair. "But there aren't enough of us with Drew laid up."

"Why? How many do we need?"

"Four couples at least - ow, Meggie, that *hurts!* At least four, if we want to dance quadrilles."

"We must have enough." I counted on my fingers. " You, me, Mama, Aunty Dot. That's four. Papa, Uncle John, Walter, Angus. *That's* four. So what's the problem?"

"Uncle John doesn't dance. He plays the fiddle." And then, in response to my puzzled look. "Who d'you think provides the music, Sarah?"

"Oh, yes. I hadn't thought of that."

Martha was silent while Meggie tied up her hair with a red velvet ribbon. Then, "I don't know why we're even *bothering,* if we can't dance! Concert night's pretty boring if that's all we do."

"Wouldn't be able to dance with Drew in any case." I said, while Meggie began the attack on my short curls.

Martha pulled a face. "Walter or Angus. Not much of a choice, is it?"

But I kept my thoughts to myself.

After Meggie had left, Martha opened a drawer in the dressing table

"Look!" She showed me a handful of pink and red petals. "I picked them this afternoon."

"What are they?"

"Geranium petals. You rub them on your cheeks."

"What for?"

Martha was applying the petals to her face, leaving a red smear on her skin.

"Gives your cheeks a bit of colour. I read about it in a magazine. What do you think?" She turned around. She had rubbed the colour into her skin where it showed as a faint blush on her cheeks. "You want some?"

I shook my head. "It'll be all right until you start sweating. Then it'll all run down your face."

"Sarah! *Horses* sweat. Men perspire. Ladies merely glow."

I grinned. "Well, when you start *glowing*, it'll run down your face. I don't think there's all that much difference myself. Now, are you ready?"

The drawing room had been arranged for the concert with a stage area at one end, backed by old velvet curtains draped over the picture rails, and a little semi-circle of seats at the other. The thick damask curtains had been released from the heavy silk ropes that held them open and were pulled across the windows to shut out the rain. Extra lamps had been brought in creating a glowing light in which even a plain girl without geranium petals on her cheeks could look like something special.

By the time Martha and I made our entrance the men were already assembled, resplendent in evening dress. Dressed in a cream silk shirt and a black velvet jacket, Drew lay on the couch looking wonderfully pale and romantic, as only Drew could. Walter was standing on the other side of the room talking to Papa but he came over when he saw us.

"Ladies."

He offered us an arm apiece and escorted us to the group of chairs. But Martha took herself off to perch on the end of Drew's couch, leaving Walter and me alone together, as neat a piece of work as I'd ever seen in my life. Looking pleased with himself, Walter found me a chair and sat down next to me.

"You look beautiful, Sarah."

"So do you."

He did, too. His high, starched collar accentuated his narrow features and dark eyes. His thick wavy hair was long enough to curl on his collar, something which was causing arguments between him and his mother. Of course, I was on his side. I liked boys with long hair. Especially tall, dark, handsome Victorian boys like Walter Greenaway.

"Girls from the future can be very forward," he said. "I'm not so sure I like it."

I grinned. "You'll get used to it."

At Marthas's insistence, the concert started with her piano piece. "Mephisto Waltz Number One by Liszt," she announced, sat down hurriedly on the piano stool and proceeded to play the familiar music. It was the best performance I'd ever heard her give, improved no doubt by the mellow quality of Grandmamma's lustrous baby grand which sounded nothing at all like the old upright in the front room at home. At the end she stood up, niccly flushed, to take her bow.

"Thank you, dear, that was very good." Grandmamma nodded approvingly at Martha. "You'll make a nice little pianist, if you keep working hard. It's such a pity dear Anne's so unwell. Otherwise we could have enjoyed some of *her* playing this evening."

"Mean old cow," I whispered in Martha's ear.

Uncle John was next. He was wearing a threadbare dinner jacket, a floppy bow-tie and a pair of elastic-sided riding boots. He took out an old violin, tucked it under his chin and launched into song.

> *"Oh the springtime it brings on the shearing*
> *And it's then you will see them in droves*
> *To the west country stations all steering*
> *A-seeking a job off the coves.*

And now the chorus! *With a ragged old swag on my shoulder* . Come on, now, join in!"

"Uncle John only ever sings shearing songs," Martha whispered. "I think we know them all."

"He's as bad as Angus. His stuff's all about droving and horses."

"It's just as well we've got Walter to sing about something important. He and Aunt Dot always do love songs, don't you, Walter?"

"Well, I suppose shearing and droving have their place in a place like Toowoomba," smiled Walter, clapping vigorously as Uncle John came to the end of the song. He leaned close enough to brush my ear with his lips. "I'm going to sing just for you, you know that, don't you?"

"I'll blush, if you do. I know I will."

"That's something to look forward to. If I sing and you blush I'll be the happiest man in the colony."

Aunt Dot took her place at the piano. She was looking very pretty in a cream hail-spot voile dress with her dark hair swept up in shining coils. She placed her hands on the keys and looked up at Walter who was leaning one-handed on the piano, the other tucked casually in his trouser pocket. He reached up and scooped his heavy dark hair from his forehead and smiled down at her.

The first soft chord was drowned by a heavy knocking at the front door.

"Now, who can that be at this hour?" Grandmamma turned her head.

We heard the front door bang, voices in the hall and then the drawing room door opened and there stood a young man in a stiff blue policeman's cape, dripping water all over the polished floor.

Martha jumped to her feet. "It's Jimmy! Oh, goody. Now we can dance!"

"Never mind dancing!" said Grandmamma. "The poor boy's soaking wet. I'll get him dried off and then I think we'll have our supper."

Mrs Armitage had laid a huge cold supper on the dining table in the room next door. There were sliced cold meats, fresh bread, pickles, cakes and tarts and a dish of beautiful fresh peaches sent over from *Westerways* by Mrs Beauchamps.

"It's a pity Estelle couldn't be here," said Grandmamma, looking significantly at Walter, "you could have given her our thanks."

Walter was peeling one of the peaches very expertly with a small pearl-handled knife, cutting it into segments and dropping the sweet, juicy pieces one by one onto my plate. "Concert night is family only, Grandmamma. Your rules not mine."

"Oh, I beg your pardon. Am I interrupting something?" Jimmy had been eating steadily ever since he sat down and now paused and looked up, his fork halfway to his mouth.

"You don't count, Jimmy. You're family enough," said Martha.

"I hear you're joining the Drayton constabulary, young Jimmy," said Uncle John. "Going to lock us all up for sheep-stealing, are you?"

Jimmy grinned but could find nothing to say.

"When do you start, dear?" Grandmamma rescued him.

"End of the month after I pass out from the barracks. I'm looking forward to it. Oh, my word I am."

Papa leaned forward. "I hear they've got the electric lights turned on in Brisbane."

"All along the street *and* in some of the shops. You should see it! Makes night look like day. There's people parading up and down until all hours."

Mama sniffed. "I should think we get enough light in the day without wanting it at night too."

"Ah, well, you might as well get used to it, Aunt. It's the coming thing. You mark my words!"

Papa's eyes sought mine. "I dare say you're right, Jimmy. We can look forward to wonderful things."

"You are going to feel like dancing afterwards, aren't you, Jimmy?" said Martha. "We need you to make up the set."

Jimmy's eyes sparkled. "That'd be wonderful!"

"We can, can't we, Grandmamma?"

"Perhaps at the end of the concert."

"Oh, who wants to hear that old stuff again! We've all heard it a hundred times before. Let's dance! Everybody wants to."

The dining table with its ruined feast was pushed back against the wall, the big cedar doors between the two rooms folded back and the chairs shoved out of the way. Grandmamma sat at the piano with Uncle John standing next to her. We took our places in square formation: Papa and Aunt Dot, Mama and Walter, Angus and Martha, Jimmy and me.

Uncle John lifted his bow. "First set! *Old Bush Barn*." and began to play.

Later there was a pause in the dancing. Someone had drawn back the heavy drapes and opened one of the French doors to let in the damp, cool air. Outside the rain still fell.

Mopping his brow with a cotton handkerchief, Jimmy walked over to the window where I was standing.

"I'm very pleased to meet you at last, Sarah. I've heard a lot about you from the girls. Daisy asked me particularly find out how you are."

"You can tell her I'm very well. And please thank her for her letter. How's Arthur Duncan?"

Jimmy snorted. "Oh, that's all over! Lizzie's got her eye on some other poor sap. Arthur's heartbroken. I told him he was well out of it. Can you imagine being married to our Lizzie?"

Walter came up carrying two glasses of lemonade.

"How are you, Jimmy? I hear you nearly gave Drew a horse-whipping when you were up here?"

Another one of Jimmy's bashful grins. "Hardly a horse-whipping, Walter."

"No more than he deserves, in any case. You've heard what happened to him, I suppose?"

"I saw him upstairs when I was getting changed. He lent me these clothes. He doesn't look at all well. Will he be all right, d'you think?"

"He'll live to dance another day."

"But tonight it's my turn! I can't believe my luck arriving on concert night. And dancing with such attractive young ladies."

"Sarah is looking *very* well," Walter agreed, handing one of the glasses to me. "She's been riding every day. With Angus Buchanan. Have you met Angus yet? A fine chap."

I dropped my head to avoid the laughter in my lover's eyes. He was teasing me, a new game invented that morning.

"Don't spill it," he said, reaching out and touching my hand.

"D'you think he noticed?" I asked when Jimmy had wandered off to get a drink for himself.

"Noticed what?"

"Us. I always think we look a bit obvious."

He shook his head. "I don't think anyone notices. They just think how *nice,* Walter and Sarah are talking to each other. Oh, look, they're talking to each other again! They wouldn't know what love was if it jumped up and bit them on the nose!"

I giggled. "Poor things."

"Yes, it is sad, isn't it? D'you want to come and help me in the kitchen?"

"What are you going to do in the kitchen?"

"I thought I might get some more lemonade. I'm sure we must need some."

Walter took the cup out of my hand and dumped it on the nearest chair.

Hand in hand we ran along the covered way between the silver curtains of the rain. The kitchen was dark and warm, smelling of the fresh bread left to prove in a big earthenware bowl on the table. Walter kicked the door shut with his foot.

We made our way around the big table and found the old armchair by the stove. The fire had been banked down for the night but there was enough heat left to caress our legs and banish the damp air. The rain played a tattoo on the tin roof above our heads.

Walter sat down and pulled me onto his lap. "I didn't like the way Jimmy Sangster was looking at you, Kirsty."

"What was wrong with it?"

"He admires you, that's obvious. I might have a rival."

"Jimmy's nice. I like him." Said to tease. And because it was true.

"I've got something for you. Hold out your hand."

Walter reached into his pocket and placed something in my palm. In the dim light from the fire I saw an ornate rose-gold locket on a heavy chain that slithered cool into my hand like running water.

"I was going to give it to Estelle Beauchamps at the New Year's Ball. I had it all planned. What I was going to say and everything. I don't know why I didn't. Here, let me put it on for you."

Walter fastened the chain around my neck and I felt the locket settle warm against my skin.

"Now kiss me!"

I did

"I love you, Kirsty."

"You don't need to sound so surprised."

"I didn't expect it to feel like this."

"Neither did I."

"You do love me, don't you?"

I twined my arms around Walter's neck. "Of course I do."

"Say it!"

"I love you, Walter."

"For ever?"

But I didn't reply. How could I? I only held him tight, shut my eyes and hoped that 'for ever' would mean what we wanted it to mean.

The music had started by the time we got back and Walter was quite right, nobody noticed we'd been away except that they needed us to make up the set. Outside the rain was coming down heavier than ever, drumming on the tin roof of the verandah and gurgling in the broken drainpipe at the corner of the building.

The boys shed their jackets, followed by their collars. Martha and I kicked off our shoes and danced in our stocking feet. Aunty Dot and Mama whirled up and down the room shedding hairpins until their hair hung in damp coils down their backs.

Towards morning the rain stopped. The windows became squares of pale grey, dimming the yellow candlelight. Uncle John lifted his bow. *"Eumarella Shore!"* and we danced the Stockyard, the very last dance of all.

When it was our turn, Walter and I danced down the length of the room between the rows of clapping hands, arms tight around each other, fingers locked and, oh! if it could be like that for ever!

But we were going home in two days and, by the end of the week, Walter would be gone.

10

The following morning Angus received a draft from his bank and took himself off into town to get kitted out for Melbourne. When he returned I was in the drawing room trying to arrange some flowers elegantly in a cut glass vase. Angus was wearing a dark suit and a high-collared white shirt that seemed to be strangling him. He went straight across to the bell-pull to ring for tea and flung himself down in a chair by the window.

When the tea arrived I poured and went across the room to hand Angus his cup. Drinking tea in the drawing room wasn't something that Angus did very often and it didn't suit him. He sat upright on a small carved chair with the saucer engulfed in one big hand, put the cup down on a little table beside him while his finger went inside his collar to tug at it uncomfortably.

I thought of the first time I had seen him in his too-small school jacket blundering his way into the railway carriage and said on a sudden impulse, "You don't have to go, you know, Angus. Not if you don't want to."

He stared at me blankly.

"To Melbourne, Angus. Don't *go*."

"I dunno, Sarah. I was never all that keen on going. All I ever wanted to do was to go home to *Richmond* station. But my father said I needed a profession. I'm a younger son, see? My brother will get the property one day and I'll need a way to make a living. And then, when I thought I might have a chance with you, I was happy to go. I thought maybe you would prefer Melbourne to anywhere else, seeing it's where you come from. A nice house. Shops. Art galleries and concerts. Girls like all that sort of thing, don't they? My sister's been in Europe for two years and that's all she ever seems to do. I had it all worked out. But now ..." He shook his head.

"There'll be girls in Melbourne. You're bound to meet someone you like."

"I don't like girls much. Not usually. I don't want some pretty, frippery creature with gloves and … and hats and all that sort of thing. They frighten the life out of me, to tell you the truth. What I want is someone I can talk to and show things to. I keep on thinking what it would be like to take you up to *Richmond* station."

He sat back in his chair, stretching out his long legs across the carpet.

"I know just what it'll be like now, after the wet. The creeks running. The grass thick and green. Walking the horses through country that goes on for ever. Three days to the wet country where the birds are. Camping by a billabong with the flocks of ducks and geese coming in to feed. And so many cockatoos and corellas they turn the trees to white." He sighed. "And chasing the mobs across miles and miles of open country. That's good fun too. Rounding them up and penning them ready for market. Going with the drovers for a couple of days camping in the bush until they reached the stock routes. Did that every year when I was a little fellow."

"What happens to them then?"

"The drovers walk 'em to Adelaide. A couple of months, if they're lucky, and hope they've still got a bit of condition on them when they get to the other end."

"Didn't you ever go with them?"

He shook his head. "No, never. I'd like to, of course I would. But, by the time I was old enough to go, I got sent to Ipswich, didn't I? To get an *education.*"

"And now you're off to Melbourne."

He put his cup down and stood up, stretching until his bones cracked and then went to the window and stared out. "I suppose I am," he said gloomily. "They say it's a very nice city, Melbourne. I expect I'll get used to it."

In the morning, Angus had disappeared and with him the mad, black mare that he called Bess, replaced by a neat pile of flimsy

132

one pound notes which had been his train fare south. Jack said there were some blokes staying at the hotel in town who were leaving that very morning to pick up a mob of cattle from the railhead at Warwick and take them to a property up north and how much did we bet that Angus had gone with them?

I didn't need to bet. I knew. I had found his battered poetry book under my pillow that morning with a gum leave stuck in it at a certain page and it wasn't too difficult to work out which poem I was going to find when I opened it up.

Angus had drawn a pencil line under part of the poem: *Clancy's gone to Queensland droving and we don't know where he are,* and in the margin, very small, the words 'don't tell' which, of course, I never did.

Although it probably would have been easier for Papa if I had because he was the one who had to telegraph Angus' parents to tell them he had gone missing.

The following day it was our turn to leave. Mrs Armstrong cooked us a hot breakfast which nobody felt like eating. Afterwards we all went off to our rooms to put on our best clothes. Struggling into our starched muslin dresses, Martha and I could hear little Ethel in the next room shouting her disapproval at being crammed into the cream satin hand-smocked frock that her grandmamma had been sewing all summer. Ethel had been allowed to spend the holidays toddling around the kitchen quarters in a cotton shift and was not keen on finery. I must admit I couldn't see much sense to it either on a steamy Queensland summer morning. My dress was already wilting in the heat and we still had the sooty train ride to go.

Meggie carried the little girl out to the front door hiding her own blotchy, tear-streaked face under a jaunty black straw bonnet trimmed with a bunch of artificial cherries. I had seen her slip out of the house after breakfast, presumably to say her farewells to Rory O'Neil. I caught the eye of my own beau, resplendent in a dark suit and stiff, high-collared shirt and received a quick private smile in return. He was saying good bye to the whey-faced Anne who had drifted downstairs in a crumpled nightdress to see us off.

Just as we were leaving for the drive to the station, Drew called out from the drawing room where he was sprawled on the sofa with a rug over his knees. "Hey, Sarah! Come 'ere."

"How about a good-bye kiss?" he said, looking up at me. "You wouldn't like me to pine away, now, would you?" And then, taking my hesitation for shyness. "Come on Sarah! There's nobody here. They're all out the front. Counted 'em going past the door." His eyes gleamed.

I bent down to kiss him quickly on the cheek but he reached out his arm, wrapped it firmly around my neck and drew my lips onto his own.

"There! That's for the kiss by the washpool that we never had but we got into trouble for anyway. And for the kiss in the paddock that I don't remember but everyone keeps telling me about. A fair dinkum kiss to keep us both going until we meet again."

"You're going to boarding school," I said. " Or hasn't your grandmother told you yet?"

"There's always the holidays, sweetheart. Long and hot, like the ones we've just had."

Drew was obviously feeling better.

By the time the train pulled into the station we were all tired and dirty from the journey. There to greet us was the heavy humidity of an Ipswich summer afternoon. The sky was covered by a thin grey blanket of cloud. Thunder muttered somewhere beyond the hot streets.

At home we found that Aunty Bet Sangster had been in, lit the stove and left one of her well-named fowls seething in its own yellow fat. On the table was a bowl of tomatoes and a fruit cake in a battered tin commemorating Queen Victoria's jubilee.

She had opened all the windows and propped open the back door - something you could do quite safely in nineteenth century Ipswich - but still the house smelt musty and unused. It seemed very cramped and crowded after *Penzance* with all the heat of the day locked in under the roof.

Outside was little better. Mosquitoes zinged and stung. The smell of the city hung in the air - wood smoke and horse dung and drains. Lightning made a half-hearted show in the clouds behind the school's roof.

Walter and I sat on the bench outside the front door, his strong fingers linked with mine. Inside, Martha was plunking away at the piano which was badly out of tune after a summer's neglect. Ethel was wailing miserably from her cot upstairs. Bertie was arguing with his father about whether he was allowed to go up the street to see his friend's pet rabbit.

"Three more days," said Walter. "What are we going to do with three more days?"

I shook my head miserably.

He leaned over and kissed me gently. "Don't be sad, sweetheart. It's not for ever."

"How do you know it's not for ever?"

"I'll be back next Christmas. I know it's a long time to wait. But I'm going to try and come up in the middle of the year if I can get some tutoring work ... What is it?"

"Don't leave me, Walter, please! I don't know what will happen to me if you go." I flung my arms around him and buried my face in the hollow of his neck.

Already it was worse than it had been at *Penzance* where it was just the planes and the traffic, far away. Since I'd been home I'd heard the TV burbling away in the corner of the living room. The click-clack of computer keys behind the closed door of Papa's study. The muffled sound of a mobile phone playing some ridiculous tune. In this house the membrane between my own world and the world in which I lived seemed dangerously thin.

Walter dislodged me and took my face in his two warm hands.

"You look pale, Kirsty. Tell me what's wrong."

I dashed at the hot tears flooding my cheeks. Took a deep breath. "When you come back from Sydney. How do you know I'll be here?"

"Of course you'll be here! Where else would you be?" And then, when I didn't speak, "You're talking about going back to your own time, aren't you? Is that what you want to do?"

"Of course I don't want to go back! I want to stay here with you."

"So what's the problem? I don't understand."

"It's just that ..." My hand crept up to the rose-gold locket I wore around my neck. "I'm not here in the same way you are, Walter, and I have to make a conscious effort to stay. It's *hard* making that effort day by day. Sometimes I wonder how long I can keep it up."

"And you're afraid that you'll just ... disappear one day, like you did when you came here? Is that what you're worried about?"

"Yes, that, and ... oh! Walter, I don't know where I might end up."

"But you'll just go back to your own time, surely?"

"I don't know that. Not for sure. That's what frightens me the most."

" I don't know what I can do to help you."

"Nothing. There's nothing you can do. I just wish you didn't have to go to Sydney, that's all."

Walter ducked his head and stared into my eyes. "Listen, Kirsty, if anything happens - if you're worried about something - write to me. Send a telegram, if it's urgent. I can be here in a day."

"Thanks, Walter."

"It's not much, I know. But it's the best I can do. Now turn your head for a moment. I've had an idea."

I felt Walter pick at the latch on my gold chain. Felt the chain move against my skin like cool water. The locket fell into his outstretched hand.

"I'm going to ask Papa to put our photographs inside. You and me. What do you think?"

"Does your father know about us? I thought it was a secret."

Walter grinned. "I think he's got a fair idea what's going on." His hand closed over the gold oval. "Don't worry, sweetheart. I'll let you have it back before I go."

When you are young and in love three days is an eternity, until they are over. Then they are nothing at all. For those three days Walter and I filled up that little house with our love.

I sat at the kitchen table sewing buttons onto his shirts and biting off the cotton with my teeth while he sat whistling through his teeth and reading the newspaper, our feet touching under the table. He went over to the school to mend the latch on a window in the boarding house and I went too, to hand him nails and kiss his thumb when he hit it with the hammer. I helped Meggie by running errands into town and Walter ran them with me. He didn't seem to mind carrying the basket which we filled with bread and potatoes and parcels of meat. Then we'd buy a pennyworth of toffee and walk back slowly along the river where the old wharves were.

One time we climbed down the steep wooden steps and sat on the hot timber of the wharf with our legs hanging over the brown water and our hands laced tightly together, talking about where we were going to live when we got married and how many kids we'd have. The usual nonsense. I tried his name out on my tongue. Kirsty Greenaway. Which didn't sound too bad. Except that it would be Sarah.

And on the very last afternoon when there was nobody in the house but Meggie singing in the kitchen we stood together on the half-landing of the stairs with the coloured light falling all around us and promised that we would be together for ever, even if it was only in our hearts.

The next morning it was pouring with rain. Walter and I walked down to the station huddled underneath an old black umbrella. We went down the hill behind the railway yards and walked along the river where the deserted warehouses and shipping offices sat miserably under the weeping sky.

There was a narrow lane behind a row of warehouses, the entrance hidden by the drooping leaves of a Moreton Bay fig. It dipped down between stone walls and ruined wooden fences until it came to the railway line where there was a stone archway leading underneath. It was damp and gloomy in the tunnel, smelling of dirt and coal smoke, but the rain didn't get in and it was dry underfoot. Walter folded up the umbrella and shook it firmly. He leant it up against the stone wall at the entrance to the narrow tunnel. Then we went into the musty, damp-smelling darkness and kissed for a long time.

When we came up for air, he said, "Will you write?"

"Of course I will. Every day. Will you?"

"Perhaps not every day. And you'll let me know if anything's bothering you?"

I nodded. I wasn't going to cry. It was bad enough as it was.

"You'll come home? If I need you."

"Yes. Of course I will." Walter's face was creased with anxiety. "Promise?"

"Cross my heart." He kissed me again and went to retrieve the umbrella. "Now, come on or I'll miss my train."

When we arrived at the station the locomotive was already wreathed in steam which lingered in white wisps under the canopy of thick grey clouds. Neither of us had any desire to prolong the agony so Walter shook me firmly by the hand, leaving an impression of his warm fingers against my skin to match the memory of his lips against mine, handed me the umbrella and climbed on board.

Just before I turned away I looked up and saw his face, as dearly familiar as if I had known him all my life, pressed up against the grimy window, his eyes searching for mine across the several feet of wet pavement that separated us.

It wasn't until I'd watched the train disappear into the rain murk that I remembered Walter still had my locket.

Grey dawn arrives slowly. It has rained all night. Outside my window water drips onto the concrete path. Above my head the fan hums quietly, shifting the damp air. With the end of the long night in sight I fall suddenly into a deep sleep, waking some hours later, dazed and groggy. On the bedside table, the diary lies where it fell last night, its old pages spotted with mildew. The memories flood my mind. Tears are very close. But I won't cry. Not yet.

In the dining room I walk around the walls, examining the photographs. The family party on the back lawn. I remember Jack and Bertie with the tails of their sugar mice hanging out of their mouths, hoping Papa wouldn't notice. Strange to think of them dead in the trenches at Gallipoli.

The photo of Angus and me with the horses. I had forgotten how much weight I had put on with all the stodgy food we ate and no exercise. Mama called it puppy fat and was pleased she had been able to fatten me up. They had different ideas of beauty in those days.

By the door, I stare at the photograph of the young man that Greg thought looked like him. I know who it is. It isn't Drew. It is Walter.

I touch my finger to the cold glass. Oh, Walter, where are you?

But I know the answer only too well.

Everyone was in the kitchen, sitting around the remains of a bacon and egg breakfast. In the corner, the mutter of the radio.

"Ah, you're awake!" said Mum. And then, "Kirsty, what's *wrong?*"

"Nothing, why?"

"You don't look very well. Didn't you sleep?"

"I've just got a bit of a headache, that's all."

"D'you want a cup of tea?" asked Allie. "There's fresh in the pot. And hot bread out of the machine."

"We've been waiting for you to wake up," said Greg. "You'll never guess what we've got. Lottie's papers!"

Lying in the middle of the table was a battered foolscap envelope. On the front in thick marker pen was written the name 'Hall, C. S.' and a file number. A series of seals decorated the opening.

"Do you want to open it?" asked Mum.

I stared around at the wall of faces.

"No. Somebody else can do it."

Allie reached for the envelope. "Shall I? Here goes!"

The contents slid out onto the bench among the breakfast things. There was a faint smell of dust and mothballs. David reached out his hand for a flat, grey box half hidden under the pile of yellowing paper and dog-eared envelopes.

"Here you are, Kirsty. Open it."

"What is it?"

"I have no idea. Open it and find out."

Inside, lying on faded red silk, was a military medal made of some dull metal, hanging from a coloured ribbon.

I looked up at David. "What is it?" I said again.

His hand came forward eagerly. "It ... it looks like a Victoria Cross. Turn it over, Kirsty."

I lifted the medal out of its box and held it in my hand. Turned it over and read the inscription on the reverse side.

Posthumously awarded to
Lieutenant Andrew John Greenaway
for exceptional valour in the face of danger.
Ypres, France. August 1916.

"Andrew John Greenaway? *Drew!* It's Drew's." I stared around the table. "What does 'posthumously' mean?"

David leaned forward. "It means whatever he did he died doing it."

Drew the hero. It was a strange concept. I looked down at the medal lying cold and solid in my hand. Remembered Drew the last time I had seen him, lying pale under a rug and the devil in his eyes. Remembered him on the back of that mad black horse. Remembered him at the washpool with his hands resting on my shoulders. They had been so warm, those hands, against my cold, wet skin.

"Poor Drew." I dropped the medal back into its box and passed it across to David's eager hands.

Allie reached out for a thick envelope with 'Marriage Certificate' written on the front in faded ink. Inside, a piece of paper folded into three upon which a dark-red rosebud had left its impression. She unfolded the paper and handed it across the table to me.

"Come on, Kirsty! Read it!"

I took the paper in my hand and stared down at the faded writing.

On the 26th August 1929 Thomas Arnold Hall and Charlotte Sarah Greenaway had been married in the Presbyterian Church, Drayton.

140

Allie leaned across and took the paper back. "So she was a Greenaway after all!"

"All we need now is Lottie's birth certificate so we can find out who her parents were," said Mum. "Anybody want to have a guess?"

David took off his glasses and polished them thoughtfully on a clean handkerchief out of his pocket.

"If Anna di Allessi - Anne Greenaway - was the last of the family, it doesn't leave many candidates, does it?"

"I'm still keen on my theory," said Greg. "About Lottie's mother anyway."

He was trying to catch my eye but I refused to look up. I knew, after all, who Sarah was. What I didn't know was what had happened to her ... to me. And I wasn't sure I wanted to find out with all the eager, cheerful faces watching for my reaction.

David sifted through the papers scattered on the table. A bundle of letters tied up with pink ribbon. A few curled up photographs, faded to brown. Lottie's red rosebud fell apart, scattering crimson fragments.

The birth certificate was a brittle piece of yellow paper, torn on the corners. David picked it up between thumb and finger.

"Here we are. The moment of truth!"

I watched as he opened it up and smoothed it with his hand. He handed it across the table to me. It was written in faded handwriting and was hard to make out.

Charlotte Sarah Greenaway.
Born 23rd March, 1906.
Father: Walter John Greenaway.
Mother: Estelle Mary, nee Beauchamps.

It was like a punch to the stomach.

As if from a distance, I listened to their excited voices.

"Walter! So it was Walter all the time."

"Estelle? Who's Estelle?"

"Don't you remember? She was the girl Walter was with at the New Year dance."

"Martha *said* they were going to get married!"

"What do you think, Kirsty? *Kirsty*?"

I shook my head. My hand clutched the gold chain around my neck. I felt the hot tea and fresh bread rise in my throat like bitter bile.

"Kirsty, are you all right?"

"Excuse me ..."

I returned five minutes later to be met by the wall of eyes.

Allie said, "Please don't tell me it was something you ate."

"No, it wasn't the food. I think I'm just coming down with something."

Mum stood up. "I don't think we'll stay for lunch, Allie, thanks all the same. We'd better get Kirsty home."

I made my way around the table to where Greg was standing. "I'm sorry, Greg. Truly I am. None of this is your fault."

I felt his arms come around me. The familiar warmth of his body against mine was almost more than I could bear.

"It's okay, Kirsty. Take care, huh?"

It was a silent journey. David concentrated on driving on roads sluiced with water with Mum sitting upright in the seat next to him, a basket of left-over goodies squashed by her feet.

In the back seat I lay half-asleep, listening to the swish of the tyres on the wet road, while the memories scrolled relentlessly through my head. They were all of Walter. The first kiss by the billabong. The night of the concert when he told me he loved me. His warm hands on either side of my face as we sat outside the house and I told him of my fears. The last thing I could remember was Walter's face through the grimy glass of the railway carriage. After that, nothing.

It was still raining when David drove into Burnett Road and stopped outside the convenience store on the corner.

"What else besides bread and milk?" he asked Mum. "D'you want the papers?"

"Yes please. And get some chocolate, David. The sort with nuts in it."

When he had gone she turned to me. "Okay?" In that pretend cheerful voice she uses when she knows I'm anything but.

I nodded.

"I'll tell you what we'll do. We'll have tomato soup for lunch. Out of a can." She kicked the basket of food at her feet. "David can eat Allie's leftovers. Or they can go in the bin. I think we've had enough rich food to last us a good long while."

We sat in the kitchen and had our soup with a plateful of buttered toast. Then I wandered into the front room and turned on the TV. But all I could think of was Walter. The house was full of him that rainy afternoon. The smell of his tobacco drifting through the open window. The feel of his body against mine as he crushed me against the linen cupboard door for a kiss. And the small landing half way up the stairs where we had stood in each other's arms and laughed at the patterns of coloured light falling on our faces.

But there was no light today. Only grey. And no Walter either. Yet still I refused to believe that he was dead although knew in my heart that he must be. Instead I imagined him in another world, a world that I could not reach. Young and healthy and pursuing his career as a doctor. Married to Estelle Beauchamps, the dark-haired girl I'd seen at the New Year dance.

But that was not a thought I wished to dwell on. In the end I went upstairs, rolled myself in my quilt and escaped into sleep.

11

It was a tradition at my school for all Year 11 history students to take the heritage trail around Ipswich, as a sort of gentle curtain-raiser for the work that was to follow. Like most school trips, it was no big thrill but at least it got us the afternoon off and the chance for a little mucking around along the way.

Mum was not keen on me going. She said it was too hot and I hadn't been well. But I was determined to go. I knew I was waiting for something and it was driving me mad. It was the last piece of the puzzle, hovering just out of reach, tantalising me, frightening me, making me nervous and upset and unable to concentrate. And somewhere out there on the doubly-familiar streets was the trigger, the thing that would make me remember.

Ever since my return from *Penzance* I had been living in some kind of limbo between the real world and the one where Walter was. Each morning I woke too late to catch the shreds of my dreams, vivid dreams that haunted my days, inhabiting the corners of my mind where I couldn't reach them.

The house lay around me as quiet as the grave. No music. No tobacco smoke. The laughter silenced. The sunlight streamed through the round window on the stairs but it brought me no joy. Only Walter's gold chain remained as a tangible reminder of where I had been.

Like many Australian towns, Ipswich is a somewhat depressing mixture of old and new, the beautiful and the tawdry. Lovingly restored buildings cheek-by-jowl with concrete horrors daubed with graffiti. Racks of cheap clothing in the mall, picked over by fat women with babies in strollers. The smell of stale beer from the old pub on the corner. Buses and cars a barrier of noise and pollution down the main street. The sound of the post office clock hanging in the hot air. But it was not what I saw that February day.

The minibus dropped us off at the top of the hill behind the hospital and we climbed the water tower to look at the view. On one side, Ipswich crammed untidily into its bowl of land with the grammar schools on each hill and the green slash of Queens Park. On the other side, beyond the curve of the river at One Mile, flat grey country with the low hills shimmering on the horizon.

In Brisbane Street several boys left the group furtively to play computer games in the mall. I stumbled along the footpath under the wooden awnings of the old shops and the noise of the cars and buses in the street faded away to be replaced by the remembered sound of horses' hooves and the hiss of carriage wheels. The smell of dust and wood smoke filled my nostrils, together with old cabbage leaves and fresh cakes. There was another smell, too, but not one I recognized, a stench of filth and fear that lodged itself at the back of my throat and would not go away.

Then we were by the river. A roundabout, busy with traffic, the ramp at the back of the bus station, a concrete car-park. Lizzie and Daisy laughed in my ear, talking endlessly about boys and clothes. The old grey wharves crowded the river bank where bare-foot boys fished with bits of string. An electric train hurried along the track behind us and I remembered the old steam trains and Mama shaking out her skirts and complaining about the dirt. Remembered standing on the Toowoomba train with Papa, waiting for Angus to come. Remembered the pouring rain and Walter's face pressed against a grimy window.

We crossed the river, straggling along in ragged groups, teachers at either end. The sun bore down on my head to meet the heat of the pavement rising up. Beyond the city a thin grey haze was creeping across the sky, backed by white thunderheads, hazy and ephemeral. In the middle of the bridge I paused to catch my breath and found myself staring at the brown water flowing dizzyingly below me. The taste of fear rose in my throat and made me choke.

North Ipswich. Gasometer. Railway workshops. Butter factory. Hot pavements. Traffic. "Are we nearly *there?*" Teachers hustling.

Across the road. A park. Ancient trees in heavy leaf. Sprinklers cool on the gardens. The minibus parked in a side street ready to take us back to school.

A tall white memorial with a broken column standing on the dusty ground. Words carved on marble.

This memorial was erected by public subscription
to the memory of Constable James Sangster
who lost his life in a gallant attempt
at rescue in the flood waters
in the Brisbane River
5th February 1893

I staggered a little. Grabbed wildly at something to stop myself falling. Heard cries of alarm. Somebody held me and led me to a bench. Took my head and forced it, not gently, between my knees. A drink bottle was held out to me. I took a swallow of lukewarm cordial and vomited it out onto the dusty ground. I started to cry, great sobs that shook my body. Then I was shivering. Shivering and crying, as if I would never stop.

A teacher took charge. Shepherded the other kids away. I heard someone on a mobile phone, talking to the school. But my tears were a curtain, a barrier, locking me into the world of dreams, of memories. There would be no escape. Not this time. This time I would remember.

They drove me home, over the terrible bridge with the brown water beneath. Mum was there waiting. She took me inside. "Straight to bed, I think. I *told* you not to go!" Her face was a mask of anxiety. "I've got to go back out. I was in the middle of a meeting."

I had a shower. Stood while the cold water pelted on my head. Made her wait. Why couldn't she just stay home, for once? Didn't I count? Ever? But at the same time I wanted to be alone. To let the memories out. To find out finally what had happened to me.

Alone in my room, the curtains whispering at the window, the thunder clouds casting a mantle of oppression over the city. My mind free to wander. And back I went with a jolt, back to the days after Walter and I said good-bye at the station and he went away.

That Sunday night the wind had got up and, by the time Martha and I went to bed, it was buffeting the house with strong gusts that rattled the glass in the windows and threw rain in hissing handfuls down the kitchen chimney.

Martha and I crouched against the window and peered out into the windy darkness to where the yellow lights of the grammar school windows showed in patchwork against the thrashing branches of the trees.

With the new day no more than a hint of grey at the edge of the sky, we were woken from restless sleep by a tearing sound above our heads followed by a loud crash.

"What was that?" My heart was pounding in my throat.

"Sounded like slates breaking."

A few minutes later the water started dripping through the ceiling in the corner of the room and then Papa came in carrying a candle. He put the china bowl that we used to wash our faces under the drip and came over to the bed. "Go back to sleep, girls. It'll soon be morning."

Full morning showed the extent of the damage. The clouds were heavy in the sky, dropping rain in grey sheets onto the sodden ground. The wind blew in fitful gusts. A tree had fallen across the horse paddock on the other side of the road, smashing the fence. Broken slates were strewn everywhere. At the school a whole patch of tiles had been ripped off and we could see the bare timbers of the roof.

"What a day!" said Papa, eating his breakfast on the run, his collar flying. He kissed Mama on the cheek. "I'd better get over to the school. I'll try and get someone to come and look at the roof later on."

In the afternoon Martha and I went round to Wharf Street to see Lizzie and Daisy but Aunty Bet said that they had gone out to look at the river. The wind had died down by then and the rain had settled down to a steady drizzle although there was still a strange feeling in the air as if the whole world was waiting for something to happen. Cyclone weather, it was, but I didn't know it then. I had never been in a cyclone before and didn't know how you feel them in your head and in your guts without having to be told there is one around.

Angus would have said that the river was running a banker. It was a good description. The river, normally a placid flow at the bottom of a steep incline, was now a brown torrent, tearing at the trees on the far slope and threatening the pylons on the big high iron bridge that carried the railway line. High on the flood floated great lumps of timber jostling and bumping each other as the water carried them along.

"It must be the wharves! " said Martha, quickening her step.

We came to a group of people and pushed our way through. Lizzie and Daisy were at the front of the crowd with Bertie who must have run all the way from school and was red in the face from exertion and excitement.

"Have a look at this!" he said when he saw us.

The old wooden wharves were awash with brown water, the swift current plucking and tearing at the grey timber of piers and decking, breaking them up bit by bit and carrying them away.

As we watched, a whole section broke away and floated like a raft into the middle of the stream where the swifter currents spun it around, tipped it onto its side and smashed it to pieces. A derelict shed hung for a long moment over the rushing water until it, too, fell with a great crash and a flurry of water, taking with it a set of wooden steps that joined the wharf to the road just next to where we were standing.

In the silence following the shed's collapse we could hear the pitter patter of soil and rocks rolling down the slope.

Just then Jimmy Sangster came along in his new policeman's uniform, not quite sure whether to be self-important or embarrassed in front of a group of people who had known him since he was a little boy.

"Step back, ladies and gentlemen. Step back." He spread his arms and made shooing movements.

He stood in front of us, stroking his new black beard. "Hello, Martha. Sarah. How did you get on at your house last night?"

"The tiles blew off and there's a big bulge in our bedroom ceiling," said Martha. "What are you doing here, Jimmy? I thought you were going to Drayton."

"I will be when I can get through. There's a lot of water between here and the Range. You know Brisbane's flooded?"

"What about Ipswich? Are we going to get flooded?"

Jimmy looked up at the congested sky. "I don't think the river'll get much higher now. And the rain's stopping." He touched his cap with one finger. "Say hello to your ma and pa, won't you?"

Martha tucked her hand into my arm as we walked away. "I think he likes you! Did you see the way he was looking at you?"

I shook my head. "I don't think so."

"Don't you like our Jimmy, Sarah? He's only a policeman, I know. But he'll be a sergeant one day."

I squeezed her hand. "Give us a break, Martha. Come on, let's go home."

Jimmy was right about the rain. It did stop and the river went down although not to its normal placid level. The slates on our roof were replaced but Martha and I watched anxiously as our ceiling continued to bulge and bits of plaster flaked off and fell onto the floor. Papa said we weren't in any danger and the ceiling wasn't worth fixing until it had dried out thoroughly but he wasn't the one who had to sleep under it night after night.

Then, two weeks later, it began raining again. The clouds covered the sky, the wind picked up, the mosquitoes went away and we opened up the windows to let the cool damp wind swoop through the house. Papa came home on the afternoon of the third wet day, blown into the house by a freshening wind and sat down heavily at the kitchen table. He wrapped his hands around a mug of tea and blew on it to cool it down.

"There's another flood coming. They reckon Ipswich'll cop it this time as well."

Mama turned from the stove. "What are we going to do?"

"I'll tell you what I'm going to do." Papa swallowed the rest of his tea and got up from his chair. "I'm going to get the school wagon and go into town for supplies. We've sent everyone home who can get home but there are twenty boys left that'll need to be fed." He went over to Ma and put his arm around her shoulders. " We won't be flooded, my dear. Not up here. It'll just be a case of doing what we can until the water goes down."

That night when the river burst its banks Pa went down into town to help empty the shops and evacuate the low lying houses. Close to midnight he came back up to the house tired and wet. He said the water was already half way up Brisbane Street and that a brick laid in the middle of the road was covered by water ten minutes later, so swiftly was the water rising. It was a strange, silent night with nothing to be heard but the soft hush of the rain. Towards morning the rain stopped altogether and a full moon broke through the clouds, reflecting silver light on black water lying where no water had lain before.

The morning dawned grey and wet. Martha and I followed Mama across the road to the school to cook breakfast for the boys. Before we started, we climbed the twisting wooden staircase to the top of the school tower and looked with awe at a city awash with water. Grey water lay still under a grey sky, filling the hollow of land where the shops and houses were. Beyond the city rose the sharp escarpment where the new girls' school stood and Queen's Park, a lurid green against the heavy sky. On the north side, beyond the iron bridge, the gasometer sat like a metal sandcastle, surrounded by water.

"Aunty Bet's house'll be under!" said Martha suddenly. "I wonder what's happened to them?"

"Nothing we can do anyway." I turned to go back down the stairs. "We're stuck until the water goes down."

Ipswich lay under water for five days and for those five days we fed the boys, getting up at first light to make porridge, boil water for tea, and toast what was left of yesterday's bread for them to cover with butter and jam, before beginning again with another batch of bread and boiling up meat and vegetables for their evening meal.

Papa decided that the best way to keep the boys quiet was to give them their ordinary lessons and this he did, teaching them maths every day which he said they desperately needed being uniformly extremely bad at it, reading them stories in the afternoons and, to make up for the fact that they were all at school while everyone else was at home, he took them off into the little shed behind the classrooms which was all the school had as a science laboratory and showed them the sort of experiments that have a bang or a fizz at the end of them.

The result of all this enforced study was that the boys came into the dining hall as noisy and boisterous as well-disciplined boys can be when they are suffering from extreme boredom and frustration, and more hungry than they had ever been in their lives. Or, at least, Mama said they must have been. She couldn't imagine them eating that much the rest of the time.

There were a couple of senior boys - hard bush-men Papa said they were when they weren't at school - who refused to do the lessons and spent their days rowing around the city rescuing people from roofs or taking food and supplies to people stuck in isolated places. They came back to school in the evening with their boots covered in mud to eat their dinner with Papa at the top of the table and accept the glances of admiration and envy cast their way by their pale-faced school mates who had been stuck indoors all day.

These boys were put in charge of the dormitory though Papa went over to the school several times during the night to check things out. As he said to these six foot tall schoolboys, smoking their pipes in the masters' sitting room before lights-out, it was not that he didn't trust them but there were a number of shifty looking characters around who had been displaced by the flood and were wandering aimlessly around the neighbourhood begging at kitchen doors. That was the reason he slept at home and that was the reason Martha and I often saw the pale yellow glow of his lantern wobbling its way across the paddock at different times of the night.

One of these boys, Lincoln Davy, came over to the house one afternoon with a half-drowned grey kitten which he'd found up a tree. He stayed to listen to Martha playing the piano even though she said that the damp weather had ruined the tone and he shouldn't mind if it sounded terrible. Martha told me later that he had as much land as the whole of the British Isles put together and wonderful dark eyes that he'd got from a Welsh grandmother. So he was rich *and* good-looking. A dangerous combination!

On the fifth night of the flood the water left the town as swiftly and silently as it arrived, leaving behind a stinking mess of mud.

"I'm going into town." said Papa after breakfast. "I want to see if I can get over to your sister's."

"Bring them back here, won't you? It'll be a long time before Wharf Street will be fit to live in."

Where are Daisy and Lizzie going to sleep?" asked Martha. "Not with us, I hope!"

"We'll all have to do the best we can. You included, young lady!"

In the middle of the morning Lincoln Davy called in to see Martha on his way back to school. He brought gifts for Ma, too, a quarter of a pound of tea in a fat blue paper bag and a slim bottle of brandy, handed over with apologies in case he was causing offence. One of the pubs in town was open and Lincoln had been in for a beer, something which would have got him expelled under normal circumstances.

While he was there he'd heard a story which he was anxious to share with us. It seemed that the flood had claimed a victim and created a hero in the person of a young man who had drowned trying to rescue two people from a tree.

"The boat he was in capsized." Lincoln accepted a cup of tea and a thick slice of cake. "I've been in boats myself all week so I appreciate the danger. Appreciate being alive, too." He looked up at Martha.

"What were they doing in the tree?" asked Martha.

"Their house had been carried away by the flood. It was over at Kholo somewhere."

"Do you know who he was?"

"A local lad. A policeman. His name was Sangster."

"That's our Jimmy." Ma sat down suddenly at the other end of the table.

"You know him?"

"He's my nephew. My sister's boy." With a shaking hand Ma unscrewed the cap of the brandy bottle and sloshed a generous helping into her tea cup. "Drowned, you say? Are you sure?"

Martha started to cry and I put my arms around her. I was not far from tears myself. I kept on thinking about Jimmy, that cheerful, friendly boy who had died in a flood which had seemed to us no more than an adventure. I remembered him that day at the wharves with his blue serge suit and his new black beard, showing off in front of his sisters. Remembered dancing with him that rainy night at *Penzance*. I tried to imagine what it must have been like when the water took him, tugging him along remorselessly and finally pulling him down into the brown depths where there was no air.

"I'm sorry, Mrs Greenaway." Lincoln reached his hand across the table. "If it's any comfort, they're all saying how brave he was. They're raising money to put up a monument."

"Poor Jimmy. He liked being a policeman, too," Martha sniffed. Her face was red and blotchy but, for once, she didn't seem to care.

"Never mind poor Jimmy," said Ma. "What about my sister? And your uncle George?"

Half an hour later Papa arrived home with Aunty Bet. She was leaning heavily on his arm, scarcely able to walk. Her plump face was crumpled with misery. Mama sat her in the old armchair by the fire. She put a blanket over her knees, poured her a cup of hot tea and added a generous slug of Lincoln's brandy.

Meggie gave Papa a bowl of barley broth and he sat silently at the kitchen table, eating steadily while we all stood and watched.

There didn't seem to be anything else to do.

"Where's Bertie?" said Papa suddenly, lifting his face up from his plate.

Mama was sitting on a stool next to her sister's chair, soothing and petting her like a small child. She turned her head around, her face blank as if she was having trouble understanding what Papa'd said. "He's off somewhere with the lads. He won't be far."

"But, my dear, it's not *safe* out there. There's water everywhere."

"Well, he *can* swim. He spent all summer learning. That's the only reason I let him go."

"Not in that stuff he can't. Nobody can. Why d'you think our Jimmy drowned?" Pa stood up, scraping his chair on the floor. "I'd better go and find him. You stay here and look after your sister."

He moved towards the back door but it flew open before he could reach it and a young boy rushed into the kitchen.

"It's Bertie! " he cried, his eyes looking wildly around the room. "He's fallen in the river."

I grabbed hold of him. "Show me!"

"Quick!" He ran out of the door and I ran with him. I climbed over the fence into the field behind the house and ran down the hill to where the flooded river was looped in coils of brown water across the flat country and poured itself in a flurry of foam through the railings of the One Mile bridge.

"Where is he?" My lungs were almost bursting as we arrived at the river's edge where a grey cattle dog stood with his feet in the water barking at nothing.

"Look, there!" The boy pointed.

A tangle of bushes some distance from the water's edge, tugged by the current. A dark shape clinging. As I watched, one of the bushes broke away and was carried downstream. A yell of fright from Bertie and I saw his hands reaching and grabbing.

"Hang on!" I yelled, my voice thin above the roar of the water.

I kicked off my boots and pulled my dress over my head, not caring that I was standing in no more than my underwear. Frilly underwear that made the little boy by my side gasp in amazement.

I dived into the water and felt it close over my head, cold and dark. I came to the surface and felt the current tugging urgently at my body, trying to force me under. It plucked at my arms as I forced them into action, pulled at my body as I tried to get myself over to where Bertie clung precariously in the huddle of branches. Then I was close enough to see his face, white with cold and fright, and hear his voice calling to me across the swirl of water that separated us.

I reached the trees and Bertie grabbed me, wrapping his arms around my neck and forcing my head under the water. I came back up, gasping for air, and found that we were out of the shelter of the trees and moving swiftly in the current with the hurrying water all around us.

"Shit, Bertie, what did you do that for?" I yelled as the water took us and tumbled us, rolling us over and over until my lungs ached for air. Finally I was able to grab Bertie and flip him onto his back. He struggled but I had my hand under his chin and held firmly.

"Stay still, you little bugger," I hissed in his ear.

I don't suppose Bertie had been called such a name by a girl before and it shocked him long enough to get used to being where he was and realise that he was safe. Or at least as safe as anyone can be in such a situation.

"I thought you were going to save me," he gasped. "Drew says you're the best swimmer in the world."

"I *was* going to save you. From the *trees.* I don't know what I'm going to do now. "

I stuck my head up out of the water as far as I could and took a quick look over my shoulder at the shore, hardly visible through the flying spray and far enough away for me to despair of ever reaching it. Then I glanced in the other direction and realised that we were floating at the edge of the current. If I could get us both out of its grip there was a possibility that we could make it to a scoop of sandy ground I had spotted some way ahead where a tree lay fallen in the water. I was aware of a commotion on the bank, voices crying out, and hoped that someone would have enough sense to bring a rope.

The problem was that I had no strength left. The effort of swimming out had exhausted me and now I had Bertie to contend with, a dead weight gripped firmly by one hand and trailing behind me in the water. But then I thought of Aunty Bet, shivering by the fire with her boy gone for ever and the thought of Mama looking like that was more than I could bear. It was enough to keep me going until, with my arms and legs quivering with what I had forced them to do,

I took a painful gasp of air and made what would surely have been my final effort and found that we were in quieter water with the roar of the flood behind us and the fallen tree seeming to float into reach.

No rope. They hadn't thought of that. But Pa waded up to his chest in the water and gripped Bertie's arm, wrenching him out of my hand. I felt the water take me again, a vicious whirlpool that twisted my helpless body in a circle and slammed my head against a rock, barely submerged below the surface.

Then Papa's hands grabbed my arm and I found myself on the wet ground with my feet still trailing in the water. The grey dog came up to me, sniffed me cautiously then licked my face and I stared up into his friendly brown eyes. I felt Papa pull me bodily to my feet and a blanket was wrapped around me from behind. Then he picked me up in his arms and carried me up the slope to the house.

12

They put me straight to bed. Bertie, too, because I could hear him complaining loudly from the other side of the wall. But we must have slept because the next thing I knew it was broad daylight and there was bright blue sky outside the bedroom window.

But I didn't get up. I was too sick. Ma came upstairs and felt my forehead. She said I had a fever and she would fetch the doctor. The doctor came mid-morning and examined me carefully. He listened to Ma's story of what had happened.

"Over-exertion!" he exclaimed, straightening up from the bed. "You've exhausted yourself, young lady. I don't think that two or three days in bed will do you any harm at all."

Two days later I was seriously ill. The doctor came again. He consulted with Mama in careful whispers on the other side of the room.

After he was gone Mama came over to the bed. "Sarah? Is there anything you want? Anything I can get you?"

"Get Walter." My voice was just a croak. I swallowed desperately and tried again. "Walter. Tell him to come."

She looked up to where Papa was standing in the doorway.

"She wants us to fetch Walter."

Papa hurried into the room and stood on the other side of the bed. He leaned close to me. "Did you say you want Walter?"

I struggled to sit up. Watched the room dip and sway.

"He promised."

I saw the look that passed between them.

"What does she want with Walter?" Mama whispered across the bed. "What's been going on?"

"Never mind that. Walter made a promise." Papa squeezed my hand. "I'll go to the Post Office straight away."

I waited. I don't know how long. I was in some sort of black nightmare that lasted for ever and there seemed to be a steam engine in my head, thumping and hissing, until I realised it was the sound of my breathing.

Finally I woke to the sound of the front door slamming. Footsteps on the stairs. The bedroom door opens and Walter is by the bed. My heart pounds with joy. I take a breath and almost drown. A piece of his hair falls over his forehead. I reach up to brush it back but he grabs my hand and holds it tight. He leans over the bed and kisses me. His lips are cool on my burning face.

"How are you feeling?"

"Okay."

He smiles. He knows 'okay', I taught it to him.

"You don't look okay."

"I'll get better now you're here."

But I was too far gone even for Walter to save.

Very early the next morning I came back from whatever nightmare I had been in to find Walter sleeping with his head on my bed.

"Walter?"

He wakes. His eyes are red. He touches my face. Gets up and brings a flannel from the bowl of water on the wash stand. Bathes my face. But it makes no difference. The darkness is closing in.

"Kirsty. *Kirsty*!"

I am floating, lost, tossed on a roaring sea of red and black but I come back when I hear his voice. I open my eyes and search for his face.

"I love you, Walter."

"I love you, too."

I feel the hot tears well up and fall down my cheeks.

"Don't cry, sweetheart. Don't cry. We'll meet again, I'm sure of it. There's more than one way to travel through time."

"I'm scared. Hold my hand."

"Don't be scared. I'm with you."

He sat by the bed and gripped my hands strongly. Behind his head images came and went: a dead tree standing in a sea of mud; a broken city with bombs raining down; a mushroom cloud against a blue sky and people running and screaming; a hot green jungle and the sound of helicopters. He held me. Held me with his eyes and his strong hands, all I had to hold onto as the black mist closed in. Then I saw his face dissolve, saw the skull behind the mask of flesh, the dark hollows where his eyes had been, the grinning teeth, as he crumbled to dust and was whipped away into the gathering dark. And I was picked up too, his hands no longer there to anchor me, and blown away on a black wind, tossed and buffeted so that the breath was knocked out of me until, with one huge effort I filled my lungs with air.

"Mum. Mum!"

I was thrown down. Everything was still. I became aware of light behind my eyelids and opened my eyes to a patch of early morning sunlight on cream painted walls, the shadow of curtains blowing in the wind. My mother came running into the room, thrusting her arms into her housecoat, bare feet flapping on the floorboards. And the tears overwhelmed me.

She took me to hospital. They said I had pneumonia. Had had it for several days and what on earth had she been playing at, leaving it this long?

Mum couldn't understand it. "She was all right yesterday. Perfectly all right, when she went to bed last night."

Because that was the funny thing.

I was back where I started.

The middle of October.

All those months at Martha's as if they had never been, whisked away on the wings of that black storm, which may have been a nightmare after all. And, by the time I got home from hospital, my mind had closed over it and I remembered nothing.

I open my eyes. The room is in darkness. Outside, the storm is going through its paces. Heavy rain falls, bringing up the delicious smell of damp earth. My eyes are full of tears, hot tears that drip down my cheeks and soak my pillow. I turn on my side and let them fall. After a while I stop crying. I lie quietly, listening to familiar sounds: the dishwasher chugging in the kitchen, the blare of a games show on television while David waits for the News. The door opens. I turn my head. Mum stands there, silhouetted against the hall light. She walks swiftly across the room.

"I've brought you a cup of tea."

She perches on the edge of my bed and I move my legs, to make room.

"Don't lie up here in the dark, Kirsty. Come downstairs. David's cooking steak."

I reach out and turned on the bedside light. "What time is it?"

"Nearly seven. The News will be on in a minute."

"I must have been asleep for ages."

"You have been. How are you feeling?"

"Good. I feel good." I sit up. "Tell David to put a steak on for me, will you? I'll just go and wash my face."

When I reach the top of the stairs, David is standing on the half-landing. The round window is in darkness.

"Are you ready for that steak? I'm just about to start cooking."

"Yeah, I'm coming now. David ...?"

"What?"

"You're not going anywhere, are you?"

"Down to the kitchen to cook your steak, I thought."

"You know what I mean. Are you?"

"No, I'm not going anywhere."

"Good."

David lifts one arm and I walk down the stairs until he can lay it across my shoulders in that awkward way of his, as if he is never quite sure of his welcome.

On Sunday Mum, David and I drove to *Penzance*. The house sat in splendour under a glorious blue sky. Allie, resplendent in rustling black taffeta, hurried Mum and me upstairs to her bedroom where our costumes were laid out on the bed.

For Mum, a dark blue silk gown and a straw hat decorated with ribbons and feathers.

For me, not the dreaded white muslin, but a green full-length skirt and a pretty white blouse with a low neckline and leg-o-mutton sleeves that would have made Lizzie Sangster swoon with envy.

When we were dressed we stood and stared at each other for a long moment. Then Mum stepped across the room and hugged me tightly. She held me at arm's length.

"Okay?"

I nodded.

"Come on then."

Allie was hurrying through the hall. "Out the back. In the garden."

We went through the dining room and into the garden. Tables were laid out on the lawn with the staff busy amongst them with laden trays. I saw Mr Brownlow at a corner table with his wife, beaming with pleasure.

David stood behind a make-shift bar dispensing glasses of punch. He was wearing a checked shirt, a pair of moleskin trousers and elastic-sided boots, the only concession he was prepared to make towards dressing up.

"Ladies, you look wonderful!" David bent to kiss Mum on the cheek. "Have a glass of punch. It's non-alcoholic. Or at least not so as you'd notice."

I sipped the cold sweet liquid. "Where's Greg?"

"Around somewhere." David scanned the crowded garden. "Look, over there."

Greg was busy laying a table on the far side of the lawn. He was wearing a dark suit and a white shirt with a stand up collar. I saw him reach up and scoop his heavy, dark hair away from his forehead. The high collar pushed up his face and accentuated his likeness to Walter

Clear in my head I heard Walter's voice, "There's more than one way to travel through time."

Greg came towards me, threading his way through the crowded tables. I felt my heart skip and turn painfully in my chest. I waited. He reached me. He put his hands on my shoulders and grinned down at me.

"How are you, Kirsty? You look great."

"You don't look so bad yourself."

"I've got something for you. Hang on."

He dug his finger and thumb into his waistcoat pocket. Something small. The gleam of gold. He opened his hand. Walter's locket lay on his palm.

"Go on, take it. It's yours."

"*Mine?*"

"We found it in Lottie's envelope after you'd gone. Mum said to give it to you. To say thank you for all your help. She said it'd go perfectly with that gold chain you always wear around your neck. And look at this." Greg's thumb flicked open the two halves of the locket. Together we peered at the tiny pictures. "They look like you and me. Don't you think?"

www.ingramcontent.com/pod-product-compliance
Lightning Source LLC
Chambersburg PA
CBHW070038260626
47159CB00005B/2074